TRAVELIN' MAN

Lois Faye Dyer

A KISMET™ Romance

METEOR PUBLISHING CORPORATION
Bensalem, Pennsylvania

With love and appreciation to all the men in my life who have loved me and shared my fascination with fast, classic cars. My husband and his '64 Chevy Impala, my Dad and his '58 Chevy, my brother and his '56 Chevy convertible, my son and his '69 Hugger Orange Camaro. Thanks, guys, for never telling me "girls can't do that."

LOIS FAYE DYER

Winner of the 1989-1990 Romantic Times Reviewer's Choice Award for Best New Series Author, Lois Faye Dyer lives on Washington State's beautiful Puget Sound with her husband, two children, and their golden Lab, Maggie Mae. She ended a career as a paralegal and Superior Court Clerk to fulfill a life-long dream to write. When she's not involved in writing, she enjoys long walks on the beach with her husband, watching musical and western movies from the 1940's and 1950's and, most of all, indulging her passionate addiction to reading.

Other books by Lois Faye Dyer:

ONE

This is not happening! Katherine ducked behind the edge of an overturned table just in time to avoid a flying beer bottle that barely cleared her head. Her green eyes widened as she watched the bottle hit the wall behind her, and she saw amber glass and golden liquid spray across the dingy stucco. A wooden chair sailed after the bottle and smashed against the wall, knocking a crudely executed painting of a matador and a bull crooked and destroying a poster advertising tequila. *If I get out of this cantina alive,* she thought grimly, *I'm going to kill you, Bradley Stephens!*

She peered around the edge of the tabletop. The little cantina was in an uproar. The patrons, all native Mexicans with the exception of one blond American male, yelled, pushed, shoved, and slugged, both at each other and, whenever possible, at the drunken, obnoxious American who had started the brawl.

She tried to ignore the noise of splintering wood

furniture and roared Spanish obscenities and focused on locating Bradley. Her eyes narrowed as she scanned the shifting crowd, searching for the broad shoulders and the handsome face that had set thousands of American female movie-goers sighing.

I hope someone breaks that plastic-surgery-sculpted nose, she thought, *not to mention that perfectly padded jawline and those beautifully capped teeth*.

Katherine frowned, her golden-brown brows pulling down in a little vee. She didn't see Bradley. Her gaze swept over the brawling crowd, but she still couldn't find the blond actor. On the third search, she found him. He was sidling along the far wall, obviously heading for the door and escape.

"Bradley!" Katherine leapt to her feet, dodging flying fists and bodies as she tried to reach the door that led out onto the dusty street.

But if Bradley heard her, he gave no sign. He shoved a pair of grappling men out of his way and sprinted for the door, disappearing through it without a backward glance. Katherine reached the open doorway and ran outside just in time to see the white Cadillac convertible execute a sweeping circle in the town square. Bradley managed to wipe out three pushcarts and a whole line of stalls in the open-air market, wreaking havoc among the merchants and crinkling the right front fender of the Cadillac, before he disappeared in a cloud of dust down the dirt road leading west to the Pacific Coast of Mexico.

"Oh, no! Bradley! Come back!" Katherine stared in consternation at the settling dust and silently cursed her own stupidity for accepting an invitation to take a drive into the Mexican interior with the bit player in her father's current film. Young and handsome, Bradley Stephens had an ego to match his well-built body, and it had taken less than thirty minutes for her to discover that he had the brain of a three-year-old child. He'd ignored her hints to cut the drive short and instead had continued to race recklessly over roads that became increasingly rough. The afternoon sun had burned down on the car, and when Bradley finally stopped in a small village, he dragged her into a cantina and proceeded to get drunk and obnoxious. Just when Katherine decided to search for other transportation to go back to her hotel, a local patron of the bar accidentally bumped into Bradley, jostling his arm and spilling his drink. The two men exchanged insults and then blows, and before Katherine could blink, she'd found herself in the midst of a brawl.

The sunlight glared off the stuccoed walls of the cantina behind her and she jammed her broad-brimmed straw hat on her head, glancing first left and then right as she hesitated, undecided which direction to try first. She wasn't even sure of the name of the little village. The lettering on signs and storefronts was all in Spanish and she couldn't understand a word of it. "*Policía?* Is that the Spanish word for police? No—I think that's Italian," she murmured to herself.

She stepped out into the street and began to pick her way cautiously around the edge of the chaos created by Brad's wild driving. Her white, full-skirted sundress and flat-heeled white sandals, combined with her lightly tanned skin and the blond hair tucked beneath the shady brim of the white straw hat, created a slender figure that stood out in stark relief against the swarthy skin and dark hair of the village's residents.

"Americana! Americana!" An elderly woman's shrill cry was picked up and echoed by the other merchants and they deserted their scattered merchandise to quickly surround Katherine.

"Uh-oh!" Disconcerted, Katherine stopped abruptly before turning on her heel to retreat to the relative safety of the cantina walls. But she was met with the sight of the beefy owner of the bar pushing his way through the door, followed by bruised patrons who tumbled out of the doorway after him. The frown on his face turned fiercer and he strode across the dusty street toward her, arms waving threateningly, indecipherable Spanish rolling from his lips and mingling with the shouts and demands from the crowd closing in behind her.

Katherine's heart sank. Great-Aunt Adelaide's words echoed in her mind. *Never forget—you are a Bennington and a lady. A Bennington is never afraid. And if you are, you must never admit it, and you must never allow it to show.*

So she forced herself to stand calmly in the midst of the jostling crowd. Angry as they were, none of them touched her, held at a distance by a glance from her cool green eyes and the calm sureness of her demeanor.

"I'm sorry," she said to the tavern owner, refusing to quail before his fierce black eyes beneath bushy black brows, "but I don't speak Spanish. Uhmm—*no habla—no habla español?*"

This elicited an even blacker glare from the cantina owner and an outburst of excited words and raised voices from the crowd surrounding them.

"Does anyone here speak English?" she inquired, glancing around at the angry, excited faces.

"*No hablo inglés!*" a dozen voices responded.

Oh great! she thought with a groan.

She tried again. "Police? Do you have police here?"

Again the babble of indecipherable Spanish answered her and the crowd began to move. Katherine was swept along in the midst of the people as they hurried down the street and shoved their way through a door and into an office.

Please, God, let someone here speak English! she thought.

Josh McFadden winced and shifted in the battered desk chair, trying to ease the pain in his ribs. The knife wound beneath the makeshift bandage wasn't life-threatening, but it was damned uncomfortable.

It should never have happened, he thought grimly. *The whole assignment was a fiasco.* In all the years that he'd been an agent for the United States Department of Immigration, he'd never been involved in a plan that had gone so wrong. The joint efforts of the U.S. and Mexican governments to infiltrate and break up an organization that was smuggling illegal aliens across the Mexican border and into southern California had exploded in a violent confrontation that had left Josh with a painful knife wound in the ribs, a screaming headache from a blow to the head, and numerous aches and bruises from a run-in with a smuggler who had outweighed him by at least eighty pounds.

The only consolation was that the Department hadn't lost any men. But the entire gang of smugglers had escaped, fading into the desert night as if they were wraiths.

Josh finished writing his report and tossed his pen down on the desktop, glancing around the office for the first time since he'd entered it. It was sparsely furnished with a battered wooden desk and the chair on which he sat. Across the small, stucco-walled room, two straight-backed wooden chairs stood against the wall. No pictures decorated the walls; no photos or plants relieved the stark plainness. Only a pottery ashtray, overflowing with cigarette ash and stubs, sat on top of the desk, holding down a stack of papers. A chipped coffee mug held a collection of pens and worn-down pencils.

He leaned back in his chair and rubbed a hand across his face, grimacing as his palm came away streaked with black grease from beneath his eyes. He needed a bath, some food, and about a solid week of sleep, not necessarily in that order.

A sudden babble of voices in the outer office interrupted his thoughts and he frowned at the closed door.

Now what?

He tried to ignore it, but the volume of noise increased. Obviously whatever it was was not going to go away. He couldn't avoid it. The only way out of the office and the police station was to pass through the main office, and he needed to get out of the station and down the street to Miguel Chavez's cantina. It wasn't exactly a five-star hotel, but Miguel poured halfway decent tequila at the bar, his wife was a passable cook, and the few rooms for rent above the bar contained beds without cockroaches.

He listened for a few more minutes, but the level

of noise only increased. *Oh, hell,* he thought wearily and pushed back his chair. *Maybe I can sneak out.*

He crossed the room and pulled open the door. The noise in the room was deafening. Chief Rodriguez stood with his back to Josh, facing a mob of excited citizens across the waist-high wooden railing that divided the room. The sparse furnishings in this outer office were duplicates of those in the smaller office he'd just left, the dingy adobe walls just as free of decoration. Josh propped one broad shoulder against the doorframe and folded his arms over his chest. His gaze scanned the crowd with mild curiosity, halting when the chief's broad bulk shifted and he caught sight of the woman standing on the opposite side of the railing, directly in front of the chief.

His thick lashes narrowed in surprised speculation. She was the only other American in the room. Impeccably dressed in a white cotton sundress and a broad-brimmed white straw hat that allowed only a glimpse of glossy blond hair, she was cool, calm, and collected in the midst of the crowd of arm-waving, fist-shaking, shouting local merchants.

Josh's gaze finished its slow appraisal that had started at her hat brim and worked its way down her well-curved slender shape to her feet. By the time his leisurely survey returned to her face, he found her staring at him, her thick-lashed green eyes unreadable as she watched him.

Though she appeared cool and controlled on the outside, Katherine's calm features hid the frantic butterflies that beat against her rib cage on the inside. She couldn't understand a word that the people around her were saying, but there was no mistaking the temper of the crowd. They shook their fists and waved their arms in dramatic gestures as they tried to explain their complaints to the uniformed man behind the worn wooden railing. She knew from his completely blank expression when she'd tried to insert a few words of explanation in English that he didn't understand her.

What am I going to do? she thought with near panic. *There must be someone in this village who speaks English!*

Just when she'd nearly given up hope, an inner office door opened and a man stepped through it. He stopped at the sight of the crowd before leaning casually against the door frame as if patiently waiting for everyone to finish and leave. It wasn't until the chief stepped to his right to lean closer to speak to the bartender that she got a really good look at the newcomer.

His eyes are blue! she realized with shock, and her gaze narrowed as she stared at him searchingly. He was tall, with a broad-shouldered, slim-hipped body that belonged in a men's jeans' commercial. His hair was light brown, streaked with sun-bleached strands, side-parted, and cut up over his ears in a conventional man's haircut. However, any claim he might have had to conventionality ended with his hair. Across his high cheekbones and beneath his thick-lashed eyes, so brilliant a blue that they were startling against his deeply tanned skin, were smeared streaks of dull black grease. Beard stubble shadowed his cheeks and jaw. He wore scuffed black cowboy boots and faded, skin-tight jeans. The dirt-streaked, short-sleeved khaki shirt that was tucked into the waistband of his jeans was ripped in several places, and a white bandage was visible through one of the jagged tears just over his ribs. Both his jeans and his shirt had rust-red smears and stains that looked suspiciously like dried blood. A leather gun belt with its holster buttoned closed over a handgun was slung over his shoulder. On closer inspection, she thought with dismay, he looked dangerous and intimidating, like he'd just come through a war—and lost.

She realized with a jolt that his blue gaze had moved slowly from her face to her feet and back up again in a bold, assessing sweep that brought a hot surge of color flooding her cheeks. Katherine tilted her chin and gave him a haughty glare, but those blue eyes only crinkled at the corners with amusement, the hard line of his mouth curving in a brief smile.

Damn him. She glanced away from him, but her gaze caught the still-glowering face of the cantina's bartender. *Just my luck! Blue-eyes is my only chance to find someone who speaks English.* She looked back to find him still watching her with that irritating half smile on his handsome face.

Katherine squared her shoulders, lifted her chin in an unconscious gesture of determination, and, while the police chief's back was turned, slipped through the small swinging gate in the wooden railing.

Josh watched her walk across the bare wooden floor toward him, her stride smooth and graceful, her green eyes meeting his without flinching. One long look at her had convinced him that she was someone's spoiled little rich girl, and since he spoke Spanish fluently, he already knew that she'd been dumped by her escort after a brawl in the cantina. He also knew that her erstwhile companion had wrecked the cantina and half of the market stalls and, since the man in the Cadillac had gotten away, the merchants wanted her to pay for the damage.

"Good afternoon," she said politely.

Josh felt the slightly husky, well-modulated tones feather up his spine and trigger a reaction that he would have sworn his tired body was incapable of producing. She had a voice that conjured up visions of silk sheets and naked bodies, and its smoky flavor was at total odds with her proper dress and cool green eyes.

"Good afternoon," he replied, wondering how she managed to appear to be looking down her nose at him when he was a good six inches taller than she. He could tell she wished she didn't have to speak to him and it irritated the hell out of him.

"You speak English! Thank God!"

His gaze flicked from her relieved face to the mob beyond the railing and then back to her delicate features. She was even prettier up close. He wondered briefly if that soft, smooth, honey-toned skin was a gift from nature or the result of expensive cosmetics.

"I take it you don't speak Spanish?" he asked.

"No! Not at all. Can you tell me what they're saying?"

He looked at her for a moment, as if gauging the depth of her truthfulness, before he shrugged slightly. "They want the chief of police to make you pay for your friend's damage to their merchandise, and if you can't or won't, they're demanding that he throw you in jail."

"Jail?" Katherine's heart surged upward to lodge in her throat before plummeting to land like lead in the pit of her stomach. "Oh, no!" She glanced around the sparsely furnished office area. "Is there a telephone here?"

"Nope."

"No? Oh. Well, where is there a telephone?"

"Isn't one," Josh drawled laconically.

"There isn't one?" Katherine repeated, staring at him in disbelief.

"Nope."

Katherine was beginning to think she was talking to a Gary Cooper clone. She drew a deep breath and immediately wished she hadn't, because those amazing blue eyes flicked to her breasts before returning to meet her eyes with a glimmer of masculine appreciation. She considered slapping him but decided now was not the time to antagonize the only person in the room, maybe even in the whole town, who could get her out of this mess.

"Are you telling me that there is no telephone service in this town? None at all?" she asked carefully, wanting no misunderstanding about what she was asking.

"That's right," he answered, wishing that her dress were less respectable. She had beautiful breasts, at least what he could see of them behind the modest scoop neckline. He shifted against the wall and his ribs protested, pain stabbing him with searing heat. He winced, but the woman in front of him was staring at the crowd of angry merchants, a little frown tugging down the fine arch of her brows, and she didn't notice.

If there is no telephone, how in heaven's name am I going to get back to the coast? Her money and credit cards were tucked neatly away in her purse in the glove compartment of the Cadillac and were probably halfway back to the movie location by now.

Katherine looked back at the man leaning against the doorway and watching her. She had no choice. She had to ask for his help. It was *not* something she wanted to do.

"Then I'm afraid I'll have to ask for your assistance," she said, her embarrassment at having to ask a favor of a total stranger nearly choking her, so that the words came out cold and tinged with demand.

"Oh, yeah?" Josh drawled. Tired, hungry, hurting from the knife wound in his ribs, and emotionally hung over from the carnage of the violent encounter in the early morning hours, he was in no mood to play the chivalrous gentleman to her grand lady. Even if she did have a body that snapped his own to instant attention, green eyes he was afraid he could drown in, and a mouth that he ached to taste. "And what might that be?"

"Pay these people and arrange transportation back to Santa Rosa for me," she said. "My father is Charles Logan, the movie producer. He's filming on location in Santa Rosa and he'll repay you the moment I tell him what happened."

"Aren't you forgetting something?" Josh said in a deceptively calm voice. Her no-nonsense demand and apparent confidence that he would comply rubbed him the wrong way. Had no one ever told this woman No?

Katherine blinked, staring at his unreadable face for a long moment, her mind racing. "No," she said slowly, "not that I know of—I think that about covers it. It's very simple really—you help me and— oh, of course." Her brow cleared as she realized what he meant. "You'll be rewarded for your efforts on my behalf. My father will be generous, naturally." For reasons she couldn't understand, she was disappointed that he wanted money.

"Of course. Money," Josh drawled, fixing her with a disgusted, weary look. "Actually, sweetheart," he said, a mocking smile tilting the sensual line of his lower lip, "I was thinking more along the lines of that magic little word your mother told you to always use when you wanted a favor."

"Magic word?" Katherine realized what he meant and felt her cheeks heat with embarrassment. " 'Please'?" she said. "And 'thank you'?"

"We'll start with 'please,' but since I haven't decided if I'll help you or not, you can hold the 'thank you' 'til later." Josh ignored her indrawn hiss of anger. He wasn't sure why he was teasing her, since he didn't intend to leave her on her own, but there was something about the woman that set his back up. "I'm sure Daddy will cover your debts, honey, but just to be on the safe side, what have you got on you for collateral?"

Katherine was furious. Of all the rude, overbearing, arrogant men she had ever met, this one took the prize!

"Nothing," she managed to get out through clenched teeth. "My purse and all my money, ID, and credit cards are in the glove compartment of the Cadillac."

Josh looked at her without comment. His face was unreadable, but inside he was chuckling. *No money? No credit cards? Daddy's little girl really was in a fix.*

"Sorry, Princess, I don't take IOU's from a

woman I don't know, especially when she happens to be the prime suspect in a local crime wave.''

Josh pushed himself upright and uncrossed his arms. He shifted the gun belt higher on his shoulder and stepped past Katherine without another word.

With disbelief, Katherine watched him shrug his broad shoulders in dismissal and take several steps away from her. He couldn't just walk off and leave her like this, could he? But clearly, that was exactly what he planned to do.

She ran after him, catching his arm to tug him around to face her. Her fingers closed over the hard muscle of his bicep and she snatched her hand away from the warm enticement of satiny skin over rippling muscle. He stood still, lifting one brow in inquiry as he looked at her.

"All right, damn you," she whispered furiously. "Just what do you want for collateral?"

Josh smiled, a predatory, purely male curving of his lips, and his lashes lowered to half hide blue eyes as he ran a stripping glance over her slim curves before raising his heavy-lidded glance to meet her shocked, angry gaze.

"Forget it," she whispered, amazed that she didn't shriek at him. She was so angry she could feel the heat singeing her cheeks. If looks could kill, the arrogant, dangerous-looking outlaw would have been dead. "I won't whore for you! I'll rot in this jail first! I don't care how long it takes to contact my family!"

Not a muscle moved on Josh's face as he watched the surge of color in her cheeks and the snap of fury in her green eyes that screamed aloud her offended pride. He felt an odd satisfaction that she'd turned him down flat. Evidently the little rich girl had her standards. Still, the mention of family brought to mind a nagging commitment that he'd shoved to the back of his mind for the past two months and refused to think about. Now it sprang to the surface, together with a wild idea for a solution. He wondered just how badly Little Miss Rich Girl wanted to get out of Mexico.

"Don't flatter yourself," he growled. "I don't want your body—not that it's not tempting, mind you," he added with a hot glance that had Katherine clenching her fists a little tighter. "But I don't need a body right now. What I need is a wife."

TWO

Katherine sucked in a lungful of air, her eyes rounding in surprise. Surely he couldn't have said what she thought he said!

"A *temporary* wife," Josh added for clarification.

He did say it! Dumbfounded and speechless, Katherine continued to stare at him.

Josh stared back. The demand was a spur-of-the-moment idea. His oldest brother, Cole, was getting married in exactly nine days. Josh loved his family dearly, but he'd had about all the weddings he could stand. His little sister, Sarah, and older brother, Trace, had both married within the past two years, and when Cole joined their ranks in a little more than a week, Josh would be the last one still single. For reasons that escaped him, his mother seemed to have decided that it was time for him to find a wife and move home to CastleRock to set up housekeeping, too. He really liked his brother-in-law, Jesse, his sister-in-law, Lily, and his soon-to-be sister-in-law,

Melanie, but all that wedded bliss was a bit too much to take at times. Especially when each wedding only seemed to increase his mother's determination to see him added to the number of happy couples grouped around her Christmas-dinner table.

The more he thought about it, the more he liked the idea of having a pretend wife on his arm when he went back to CastleRock. When the wedding was over and he left, he and the lady could go their separate ways.

"A temporary wife?" Katherine finally managed to say faintly. "You must be joking."

"Nope."

"But why me?" Her bewilderment wasn't feigned. She was completely baffled by his bizarre suggestion.

"Because you're perfect for the part," Josh answered. "You look and talk like a lady, and you've got a great body and great legs," he said bluntly, with another lightning-swift scan of his blue eyes from her hat to her toes and back again. "And you're every bit as pretty as one of my brother Trace's blondes. You're perfect."

Katherine ignored the flash of heated reaction to his words that set her nerves tingling and forced herself to concentrate on the central issue.

"This is ridiculous. People just don't go around marrying each other temporarily—why do you want to get married *temporarily* anyway?"

"I have my reasons," Josh said evasively. He wasn't sure he wanted to tell her why. At least not yet.

Katherine eyed his tall form with misgivings, suddenly reminded of her first impression that he was dangerous. "Are you in trouble with the law? Is this for something illegal?"

Josh grinned, the hard line of his mouth curving in amusement, his teeth a slash of white in his deeply tanned face.

"Illegal?" He chuckled, his blue eyes lighting with secret mirth. He wondered what she would say if she knew that he *was* the law. "No, this has nothing to do with any illegal activity."

"Hmmph." Suspicion still lurked in the depths of her green eyes. "I think a temporary marriage is an insane idea and I refuse to go along with it."

Josh lifted one tawny brow and shrugged his shoulders. "That's up to you, sweetheart. By the way, did I mention that this jail has no inside bathroom or shower facilities?"

The immediate picture that sprang to mind wasn't pleasant. Katherine's fists tightened and she bit the inside of her lip to keep from swearing at him. *A Bennington never uses curse words. Cursing reveals a lack of proper education and a sadly limited vocabulary*, Aunt Adelaide's no-nonsense voice whispered firmly in her ear.

"But then, you probably won't be in jail for more than, oh—maybe two or three weeks," he added casually.

"Two or three weeks!" Katherine squeaked. "That's impossible—my father will be here in a few hours."

"Hmm," Josh grunted noncommittally. "Or a few days—or a few weeks. It all depends on how long it takes him to find you."

"Find me?" She was starting to sound like an echo, she thought with disgust. "As soon as you tell the authorities to notify him . . ." Her voice trailed off into silence, her eyes narrowing with growing suspicion. "Let me guess. You aren't going to translate for me with the police chief unless I marry you."

"Nope."

Katherine wanted to hit him. Far more than she'd wanted to hit Bradley Stephens. She wished with all her heart that she'd never gotten out of bed this morning. But then, how could she have known that she would have a day like this one?

All right, Aunt Adelaide, she thought grimly. *Just what does a Bennington do in a situation like this?*

With barely a pause, Aunt Adelaide's brisk tones echoed in her ears. *If one is faced with a difficult situation, one must simply pull up one's socks and get on with it. There is absolutely no use crying over spilt milk.*

Oh, great, Aunt Adelaide, thanks for the advice!

"Just exactly how *temporary* is this *temporary* marriage going to be?" she said aloud.

Josh didn't miss the fury that flushed the soft smoothness of her cheeks and glittered in her emerald green eyes. She was trying to control her anger by deep breathing, an effort he definitely appreciated, for each breath she drew in swelled the full curve of her breasts against the soft cotton dress. He ought to let her off the hook and tell her he was kidding, but she obviously believed that he would force her to marry him, and for some reason, that rubbed him the wrong way. *It would serve her right if I really did go through with this*, he thought. Without the headache, various aches and pains, and the serious lack of sleep over the past three days, he probably would have told her, but he wasn't in a cooperative mood.

"A week, maybe, nine days max."

Katherine's eyes narrowed and her lips pursed thoughtfully. Nine days was much less than she'd thought.

"So basically, what you're telling me is that I can spend either two to three weeks in a Mexican jail or nine days in your company?"

"That's about the size of it."

"Great choices!" she muttered to herself, glancing away from his impassive face to the railing. To her chagrin, she realized that the entire crowd of village residents, including the police chief, was watching her and her companion with interest. The chief held a brass ring in one hand, and as he slowly twirled it, the dangling keys jingled softly.

"Make up your mind, lady. Me or jail."

Katherine glanced around the spartan office and restrained a shudder. It didn't look comfortable and was far from clean. She doubted that the cells for prisoners were any better. "I assume that this *temporary* marriage is a business relationship, and therefore purely platonic?"

Josh grinned, an ear-to-ear, full-fledged smile of such boyish charm that Katherine caught her breath in surprise.

"Sure, honey," he drawled. "I promise to fight you off no matter how much you insist."

She ignored the comment and tried for the last time to make him see reason. "Why won't you accept money instead—you can't want to be tied to me, even for nine days. You don't even know me!"

"I don't need money. I need a wife. Temporarily, at least."

"I doubt that I'll make a good wife—even temporarily,'' Katherine said stiffly. ''I can't cook, clean, or sew—I have absolutely no talent for any wifely accomplishments.''

''I'm not interested in whether you can cook or clean. All I need is someone to pretend she's married to me.'' Josh's gaze narrowed over her mutinous face. ''To pretend she's in love with me.''

''And exactly what do you mean by that?''

Josh shrugged, his broad shoulders lifting in masculine indifference. ''The usual—cling to my arm, bat your eyelashes at me, and coo when I smile at you.''

''If that's the kind of women you're used to, no wonder you only want a *temporary* wife,'' Katherine said in disgust. ''I will *not* cling, coo, or flutter my eyelashes.''

She said the words with such firm loathing that Josh didn't doubt her.

''Okay, fine, whatever. Just as long as you act like you're crazy about me, I'll settle for a good acting job.''

To Katherine's shock, she realized that they had just negotiated the terms of this *temporary* marriage. But before she could protest, Josh had turned away from her and was speaking in rapid Spanish. Katherine had no idea what he said, but the crowd's frowns turned to looks of surprise and broad grins. The elderly woman in the black dress who had first spotted her crossing the square gave her a wide smile, her dark eyes sparkling with delight and approval. Katherine managed a weak smile in return. Whatever the blue-eyed outlaw was saying to them, it clearly made them view her in a friendlier light.

He turned and crooked a finger in silent command.

Katherine obeyed him reluctantly, irritated at his arrogance. He slung an arm around her shoulders and tucked her against his side with familiar ease, and she stiffened, but allowed it without protest.

"What did you tell them?" she muttered, low enough so only he could hear. "Why are they smiling at me instead of yelling?"

"I told them the man you were with was a bad guy who tricked you, that you're innocent, and that you're my fiancée. I also told them they're all invited to our wedding."

Katherine struggled to maintain the stiff smile that curved her lips. The little old lady in black held out the fistful of flowers she'd been brandishing threateningly only moments before and Katherine took them mechanically. Clutched in front of her, the red blossoms and deep green foliage made a brilliant splash of color against her white dress. The noise level of human voices in the room rose several decibels and Katherine winced, struggling to understand even a few words out of the excited chattering.

"Silencio! Silencio!" The burly bartender lifted his arms and shouted for attention and silence. The crowd quieted and shuffled aside to allow a black-frocked priest to push his way to the front. The bartender's swift Spanish vied with interjections from the police chief, and the little priest's round face turned to first one, then the other as he listened, nodding solemnly at intervals. When at last the chief and the bartender finished and were silent, the priest turned to the blue-eyed American and questioned him in deep tones.

"Sí."

Katherine knew that meant "yes." But she had no

idea what the man at her side had agreed to. The priest turned a benign, approving smile on her and she suspected that whatever her future "temporary husband" had said yes to meant trouble for her. She returned the priest's smile and switched her gaze to the hard face just above hers.

"Just what are you telling him?" she whispered through clenched teeth.

"I told him that we want him to marry us." Josh wasn't fooled by the smiles she kept giving the beaming crowd. He could tell by the emerald sparks in her green eyes that murder was on her mind. He wondered briefly if anyone had ever made her do anything in her entire life that she hadn't wanted to do.

"But he's a real priest!" Katherine protested.

"Of course."

"But we'll really be married if he marries us!"

"Of course." Josh stared at her.

"But you said this was a *temporary, pretend* marriage!" Katherine hissed at him.

"It is."

"Then why are we *really* getting married?" she demanded.

"Because I don't trust you not to renege on your promise once we're out of here," he said with blunt honesty.

The fine-boned features of the face turned up to his reacted to the words with instant affront, and insulted dignity was easily readable in the depths of her green eyes.

"I will not—" she began.

"Shhh." Josh stopped her in midsentence, his attention shifting to the crowd. A little boy pushed his way to the front to hand the priest a document and a black leather-bound Bible. His brown eyes lit with shy pride when the priest ruffled his shiny cap of black hair in thanks before turning to speak to Josh.

Katherine watched with misgivings when the priest handed an official-looking document to the chief of police and opened the Bible. He smiled beatifically at Katherine and spoke to the man beside her.

Josh tightened his hand over the curve of Katherine's shoulder and tugged her forward until they both squarely faced the priest. The black-gowned man immediately began to read reverently from the book held open in his hands. The crowd stood silently, expectantly, watching the three participants in the tableau.

Katherine heard the rich, deep tones of the priest's voice fill the suddenly hushed quiet of the room. *This isn't really happening,* she thought dazedly. *This is a dream and soon I'll wake up and I'll be at home, in my own bed.* She squeezed her eyes tightly shut and then opened them wide. But her vision was still filled with the packed room and the expectant, watching faces. She still felt the warmth of the hard body of the blue-eyed stranger pressed against her side. His fingers still curved around the top of her arm with just enough firm pressure to keep her anchored to him. She glanced up at him. He was looking at the priest, his profile turned to her, the strong lines of brow, nose, mouth, and chin etched against the paleness of the adobe wall several yards away. Again she felt that strange, heated melting in her bones. What was it about this man? It was bewildering. Why was she standing here without complaint, her silence itself an act of cooperation?

As if he heard her question, the man at her side turned his head, his blue glance snaring hers with quick intensity. And in that moment, Katherine knew why she wasn't protesting. Dangerous as his appearance proclaimed him to be, there was something in those blue eyes that called to her, that reassured her that she was safe at the same time they sent little shivers of awareness racing up her spine.

It's only the safety I'm interested in, she told herself stoutly, steadfastly refusing to acknowledge the lure of blue eyes in a handsome face and a broadshouldered, rock-hard body that made her mouth go dry. Katherine had never considered herself a particularly sensual woman; in fact, she was so fastidious that she'd earned the nickname of The Ice Queen in college.

"Say *sí*," Josh prompted, breaking the silence that lengthened as her green eyes searched his. When she continued to stare at him uncomprehendingly, he shook her gently and tried again. "The priest is waiting—say *sí*."

"*Sí*."

The priest lifted his hand and made the sign of the cross, his Spanish words reverent and solemn as he did so.

Katherine looked uncertainly from the priest's smiling face to Josh's. He hesitated, and someone in the midst of the crowd called something in Spanish that set the group laughing. Josh shrugged, almost apologetically, and bent his head. Before Katherine realized that he meant to kiss her, his lips brushed against hers, the contact sending a surge of heat lightning through her veins. But as quickly as his mouth had found hers, it was gone and she was left to cope with the unfamiliar flash of desire that swept her.

Josh was having his own problems dealing with the strange sense of possessiveness and the need to linger over the kiss. He ignored it, chalking up the feeling to exhaustion, and caught her elbow in his hand to urge her ahead of him. The chief of police had spread the marriage documents on top of his battered wooden desk and stood patiently waiting to witness their signatures. Josh released Katherine and bent to sign his name.

Katherine peered over his shoulder. If she was going to be married, she ought to at least know her husband's name. *Joshua Nathan McFadden. A nice, solid-sounding name.*

"You're next." Josh straightened and handed her the pen.

Katherine's graceful script was artistic and feminine below the firm, black slashes of his signature. She finished signing and took a moment to scan the document, but it was written in Spanish and all she could really discern was that it certainly appeared to be official. She returned the pen to the desktop, but before she could pick up the signed paper, Josh reached over her shoulder and plucked it from the desk.

" 'Katherine Adelaide Bennington-Logan the Third'," he read aloud before glancing up at her, one eyebrow arching quizzically. "Quite a mouthful. What do your friends call you?"

"They call me Katherine," she said, restraining the urge to snatch the paper out of his hands.

"Somehow, I think I could have guessed that." His mouth quirked wryly as his gaze ran swiftly from the crown of her fashionably chic white hat to her sandals and back up her impeccably clad figure to her furious green eyes. "Well, Katy, let's get out of here."

"My name is *Katherine*," she said, the frosty coolness that tinged her tones doing little to hide the temper that sparked green fire in her eyes.

"I know that." With quick movements, he folded the marriage document and tucked it in his back pocket.

"What are you doing?" she demanded, her eyes following his movements. "I want custody of that."

"Oh, no." He shook his head, thick lashes narrowing over sea-blue eyes as he stared into her mutinous face. "I'll hang onto this until you fulfill your part of the bargain. Then I'll give it to you and sign for a divorce."

"You don't trust me," Katherine accused flatly.

"Nope. I don't trust you at all, Katy," he drawled. "That's why I'm keeping this for insurance." He patted his back pocket for emphasis before catching her elbow in a grip just firm enough to be insistent. "Now say good-bye and let's get out of here."

Katherine fumed with silent irritation all the while she smiled and repeated Josh's *gracias* to the priest, the chief of police, the little white-haired lady dressed all in black who had given her the bouquet of flowers, and various members of the crowd who moved aside to let them through.

At last they stepped through the doorway of the police station and onto the sidewalk, and to Katherine's surprise, it was dark. The sun had set while she'd been inside the police station, and golden light gleamed from windows and spilled through open doorways of shops and houses along the wide street.

"Watch your step," Josh's voice growled beside her as she stumbled over a loose rock in the dusty street. His hand tightened protectively over her elbow, steadying her, and instead of being offended, she was comforted by the polite gesture. He was a tall, broad shape looming beside her in the darkness, but oddly enough, instead of making her feel threatened, he gave her a sense of security. It was a strange feeling. She didn't know him at all, she didn't even like him, but she felt safe with him. It didn't make sense, but then, she reflected, none of the events of the past few hours made sense.

"Where are we going?" she asked.

"To get something to eat," he said briefly.

"Oh, no." Katherine stopped dead still when she realized that they were outside the cantina. "Not here."

Light poured through the open door, throwing a bar of gold across the dusty street. Josh paused and looked back at her when she halted abruptly. The lamplight fell across her face, illuminating the look of wary caution and stubborn refusal on her features.

"It's all right. Nobody's going to bother you when you're with me."

He said the words with such conviction that Katherine found herself believing him.

"If you say so." Reluctantly, she stepped forward, her fingers unconsciously tightening over the stems of the flowers she still held clutched in her hand.

Josh felt ridiculously pleased that she moved closer

to him as he pushed through the doorway and they entered the cantina side by side.

"Good evening, Joshua," the barkeep called in Spanish, smiling expansively and waving a white bar towel in their direction. "Come in, come in!"

Josh lifted a hand in acknowledgment and steered Katherine toward the relative privacy of a table against the back wall. He held a chair for her and waited till she seated herself before crossing the room to speak with Miguel Chavez.

"Congratulations, Joshua." Miguel grinned, his teeth gleaming white beneath the thick black mustache hiding his top lip. "You have a most beautiful wife."

"Yeah." Josh glanced back over his shoulder to find his most beautiful wife watching him, her green gaze flicking between him and Miguel as she struggled to understand the Spanish words. "I'm a lucky man," he said dryly. He turned back to the bar. "And a very hungry and thirsty man. What's Rosa cooking tonight?"

"Enchiladas," Miguel answered promptly. "And chalupas."

"Good. I'll have two plates of both—and beans and rice, and beer." He glanced at Katherine once again and grinned. "Two beers." *I wonder if Little Miss Rich Girl has ever tasted anything but white wine and champagne.* If not, she was in for a treat. Mexican beer was a national treasure.

"*Sí.*" Miguel grabbed two bottles in his ham-size hands and roared over his shoulder in rapid Spanish at Rosa while he opened the beer bottles and set them on the bar. "Anything else?"

"Yeah—do you have a vacant room upstairs?"

Miguel plucked an old-fashioned brass key with a piece of twine threaded through the top from a nail on the wall behind the bar and handed it to Josh. "Top of the stairs, second door on your right. Anything else?"

"Nope, that'll about do it. Thanks." Josh carried the amber-glass beer bottles back to the table with him and set one down in front of Katherine. He dropped into his own chair and tilted his bottle up, closing his eyes and nearly groaning with enjoyment as the liquid flowed wetly down his throat.

Katherine eyed the bottle with suspicion. It looked exactly like the bottles that Bradley had been emptying with slurping swiftness only a few hours before. She wasn't at all sure that she wanted to taste the stuff, and she wasn't at all sure that she was happy that Joshua was drinking it with such obvious enjoyment. Her gaze left the bottle and fastened on the disreputable-looking man lounging in the chair opposite her. His long legs were stretched out, ankles crossed, and he looked lazily relaxed. But then his eyes opened, his lashes lifting as his gaze met hers, and once again she was reminded that appearances could be deceiving. She felt a stab of uneasiness. What did she know about this man? Relatively nothing. Still, her pride refused to let him see that he made her nervous.

"What did you say to him?"

"Who? Miguel?" Josh's gaze moved past her shoulder to the bar before shifting back to her face. "I ordered some food—and beer." He glanced pointedly at her untouched bottle and quirked an eyebrow. "What's the matter? Don't you like it?"

"I haven't tasted it."

The look she gave the innocuous brown bottle spoke volumes and Josh hid an amused grin by taking another swallow of his own beer.

"Try it," he advised. "It's good."

"Hmm." Silence reigned for a long moment while she stared at him without moving and he stared back, equally still. "How many of them do you plan to drink?" she asked.

"Maybe a couple," he answered. He tilted the bottle and emptied it before shoving it aside on the tabletop and giving her a wry grin. "If you're really asking if I plan to get drunk and obnoxious like your boyfriend, the answer is no. I'm too tired."

"He's not my boyfriend," Katherine said primly, not quite able to conceal the flash of relief that swept her at his denial.

"No?" Josh leaned back to let Miguel's wife, Rosa, set a steaming platter of food in front of him. *"Gracias."* He smiled at her, waiting until she slid a matching platter in front of Katherine and bustled off to collect more beer from Miguel before he resumed speaking. "What is he, then?"

"He's one of my father's employees," she replied with deliberate understatement.

"Hmm." Josh chewed a mouthful of enchilada and took a swig of beer to douse the fire from the green chile sauce. He got the distinct impression that she wasn't telling him the whole story. "If he wasn't your boyfriend, what were you doing in the Mexican interior with him? Alone."

"You make it sound like I went to a motel room with him! We went for a drive, an afternoon drive—that's all!" Katherine stabbed her enchilada with her knife and scooped up a forkful. She shoved it into her mouth and chewed, glaring at Josh across the width of the rough table.

Josh watched her, a grin tugging at the corners of his mouth as he waited expectantly for the hot sauce to attack her taste buds. It didn't take long. Her eyes widened, shock rounding them with surprise before she gasped and choked, swallowing with a gulp.

"Water!" she wheezed, her green eyes welling with tears, one hand fanning her mouth as she sucked in air.

Josh tucked an open beer bottle into her fluttering fingers and Katherine grabbed it, tilting the amber bottle and pouring the liquid down her burning throat in a vain attempt to drown the fire.

She slapped the bottle down on the tabletop and glared at Josh, her emerald eyes shooting water-logged sparks at him.

"What *was* that?" she demanded, wiping at her watering eyes.

"Beer." He grinned at her, blue eyes twinkling at the outraged disbelief on her features.

"I know that—I meant, what in heaven's name is in this food?"

"Chiles—a little salsa. Why?" Josh asked, his attempt at innocent inquiry ruined by the full-fledged grin that tilted his mouth.

"You could have warned me that it was—hot," she said. Her mouth, tongue, and throat still throbbed with fiery heat. "Isn't there any water?"

Josh shook his head. "Beer's better. Water just makes it burn more."

"I don't believe you—that doesn't make sense."

He shrugged. "Whether it makes sense or not, it's true. Besides, the beer was probably processed before it was bottled. American stomachs aren't tough enough to handle Mexican water; if you take a chance and drink it, you play Russian roulette with turista.''

"Turista" was one of the few Spanish words Katherine knew, and she restrained a small shudder of distaste at the thought of the intestinal bug that often caught tourists unwise enough to eat food from the street vendors or drink unbottled water. She tilted the beer bottle and sipped cautiously, relieved when the liquid cooled her burning mouth. In fact, it was starting to taste almost good; she realized that she'd last eaten at breakfast and she was starving. Cautiously, she tried another small bite of the enchilada, following it quickly with a swallow of beer. It still made her eyes water, but she decided it tasted wonderful.

Josh watched her take several bites before he turned his attention to his own food. It wasn't until he had finished the last bite and drained his second bottle of beer that exhaustion hit him like a wave.

Damn, I'm tired. The lack of sleep over the past few days was starting to catch up to him. He narrowed his eyes over the woman sitting opposite him, daintily cleaning her plate. He wondered just how much of a fuss she was going to kick up over sharing a room with him. It didn't matter how much she protested, he reflected; there was no way he was going to trust her out of his sight until she kept her part of the bargain.

Katherine glanced up and caught him watching her with a look that made her nervous. Now what was he up to? She placed her fork carefully beside her plate, folded her hands in her lap, and stared back at him.

"Now what?" she asked him in a carefully neutral tone.

"Do you want anything else to eat?" he asked, ignoring her question.

"No, thank you."

"Good." He pushed himself to his feet and linked his fingers around one of her wrists, unceremoniously pulling her up out of her chair.

"Hey," she protested, half running to keep up with his long strides as he crossed the room and climbed the stairway just inside the entrance. "Where are we going?"

"Upstairs," he growled.

"I could have guessed that," she snapped back, stumbling slightly on an uneven step. "*Why* are we going upstairs?"

He didn't answer her. His grip on her wrist wasn't painful, but it shackled her to him and she couldn't tug free. Fuming, she stopped pulling against his hold and climbed the stairs behind him. He paused in front of a doorway just beyond the top step and shoved his free hand into his jeans, fishing out an old-fashioned brass key to unlock the door. Before Katherine could protest, he pushed the door inward and tugged her across the threshold, releasing her to quickly lock the door from the inside.

In one swift, encompassing glance, Katherine took in the sparsely furnished room with its old iron bedstead, rough blankets, bare wooden floors, and a washstand with a chipped, old-fashioned sink. Her gaze returned to rivet on the bedstead. She spun quickly, and found Josh leaning against the closed door, watching her.

"What are we doing here?"

"Sleeping." Josh moved away from the doorframe and walked around her to drop down on the edge of the bed. He shrugged the gun belt off his shoulder and set it on the small wooden nightstand. An involuntary grunt of pain escaped him when he bent to pull off one of his boots. He tugged the boot free and let it drop, drawing in a deep breath and steeling himself against the pain in his ribs before repeating the process with the other boot.

"Sleeping," Katherine repeated. Her wary green eyes chased from the two pillows placed side by side at the head of the bed to Josh's seated figure. "Why?"

"Why?" Josh stood and began to unbutton his shirt. "Because it's nighttime, that's why. Don't you sleep at night?"

"You know very well what I'm asking." Katherine was beginning to lose her temper. Again. "Why are we sleeping here? Why aren't you driving me back to Santa Rosa? Wasn't that our bargain—I marry you for nine days and you get me safely out of here?"

"Yup, that's the deal."

"Then why aren't we on our way to Santa Rosa?"

"Because only a fool would drive that road in the dark. And even if you're willing to chance dying, Katy, I'm not. So we sleep here and leave in the morning, after daylight." He finished unbuttoning his shirt and tugged it free of his waistband.

In other circumstances, Katherine would have been mesmerized by the expanse of tan skin smoothing over beautifully sculptured muscles. But she was distracted by the white bandage wrapped and taped around his ribs.

"You're hurt!" She moved an impulsive step toward him, one hand reaching to rest tentative fingertips against the white bandage where a crimson stain was slowly spreading. Her worried green gaze lifted to meet his.

Josh caught his breath at the sensual awareness that stroked up his spine when her fingers brushed the bandage. The worry in her eyes and the concern in her soft, husky tones were unexpected. For a long, tension-filled moment, blue eyes probed green. Who was the real Katherine Adelaide Bennington-Logan III? The cool, haughty, rich girl accustomed to getting her own way? Or this very real, warm woman filled with concern for his injuries?

Katherine's fingers trembled, the warmth of his hard body seeping through the bandage and into her fingertips, tempting her to move closer. Bewildered, she forgot to remember to breathe.

He struggled to remember where he was. Had she asked him something? *Oh, yeah.* "Just a scratch." His voice was a good octave lower than normal, and oddly husky. He cleared his throat. She was still staring at him, unmoving.

"What happened to you?"

"I was in a fight." He didn't want to tell her details. He couldn't tell her what had really happened; except for the local chief of police, no one was supposed to know what he was doing in Mexico. He managed a brief grin. "You should see the other guy."

He took a small, unobtrusive step back, just

enough to free his ribs from the soft touch of her fingers, and shrugged out of the shirt. He slung it over the grooved knob of the low bedpost at the foot of the bed. When he turned back to her, she was watching him with wary suspicion replacing the tender concern in her eyes.

"Why are you bleeding?" she asked cautiously, once again abruptly reminded of how little she knew about this man.

"Because when someone slices you with a knife, you bleed," he said succinctly.

Her eyes widened in shock. "Someone cut you with a knife?" Her voice trailed off to an incredulous squeak.

"Yup."

"Why?"

"I don't think he liked my face."

Katherine could only stare at him, speechless.

When she didn't say anything, Josh quirked an eyebrow at her and glanced significantly at the bodice of her sundress. "Don't you think it's time you got undressed?"

THREE

"Undressed?" To her vast irritation, her voice squeaked, again. She cleared her throat. "Why?"

"Don't tell me you sleep in your clothes?" Josh said.

"No, I sleep in pajamas," Katherine answered automatically, her gaze riveted on his lean fingers as he flicked open the top button of his jeans.

"Pajamas," he said slowly, his hands stilling to lie idly against the second button. "Well, now, that is a problem—since you don't have any with you and I don't have any to loan you." He propped his hands on his hips and eyed her with interest. "What do you suggest we do about it?"

The lamp on the stand by the bed lit the room with gold light, the frayed shade throwing his tall form into half shadow. The lamplight burnished the bare skin of his chest and arms with gold; Katherine stared at him, struggling to breathe. Her glance was drawn irresistibly from the tantalizing vee opening of his jeans up over the white bandage and defined muscles of his chest, over the hollow of his throat where a pulse throbbed visibly, and stroked over the sensual curve of his mouth to his eyes. The amusement she found reflected in the blue depths yanked her back to earth with a vengeance.

"*We* aren't going to do anything about it," she said with asperity, furious at the heat that flushed her cheeks. "*I* am going to sleep in my clothes."

The look she gave him dared him to say anything further, and Josh grinned, but held his tongue.

"Fine." He shrugged in dismissal and stepped aside, gesturing past him to the bed. "Climb in."

"No."

"No?" He stared narrow-eyed at her stubborn face for one long moment. "I don't think you understand," he said softly. "I wasn't *asking* if you would like to get in bed. I was *telling* you—get in the bed."

"No." Katherine's glance flicked over the room. There wasn't even a chair she could sleep in, or a rug to cushion her bones against the bare wooden floor. "I'll sleep on the floor," she said aloud, choosing the only option she saw available.

"No," he said succinctly. "You won't."

"Yes," she said just as abruptly. "I will. I'm *not* going to share a bed with you."

"You'll sleep in the bed, on the far side against the wall."

"And where will you sleep?"

"On the outside—between you and the door."

"For heaven's sake! You think I'm going to run away? In the middle of the night? Where would I go? Besides, I gave you my word to pretend to be your wife for the next few weeks. A Bennington," she said scathingly, lifting her chin with pride, "*never* breaks her word."

"Yeah, right, if you say so—but I'm not taking any chances. Now get in bed." He was running out of patience.

"I refuse to sleep in that bed with you."

Josh was tired of arguing, and with a suddenness that caught her completely by surprise, he picked her up and tossed her onto the bed. She bounced on her bottom on the mattress and quickly scrambled to her knees. Her hat had gone flying when he swung her off her feet and tendrils of her silky gold hair had pulled loose from their pins to tumble around her face. Flushed with annoyance, her green eyes shooting sparks, she was clearly, unmistakably, furious, but before she could burst into speech, Josh held up a hand to stop her.

"Lady, don't say it. If you're worried about my seducing you in the middle of the night, you can forget it. I'm too damned tired to do you justice, even if I was inclined to do so, which I'm not." *And that has to be one of the biggest lies I've ever told*, he thought with a silent groan, determinedly refusing to let his glance leave her face to stray over the picture she made kneeling in the middle of his bed.

"Hmmph," she said skeptically. But Josh met her disbelieving stare with a calm, straightforward gaze, and despite her inclinations to the contrary, she relaxed slightly. "Very well. But I'm *not* getting undressed and I'm *not* getting under the sheets with you."

"Fine." Josh shrugged wearily and winced at the unexpected stab of pain in his ribs.

"What is it?" Instantly distracted by the grimace

that twisted his features, Katherine scrambled off the bed with as much dignity as possible under the circumstances. "You're still bleeding!"

Josh struggled to ignore the tantalizing touch of her fingers against his bandaged ribs. "I'm fine," he growled in an effort to discourage her. "Don't fuss."

"Oh, sure." Impatiently, Katherine caught his forearm and tugged him around to face the lamp. "You're just fine. Of course, your blood is soaking through this bandage, but then, that's perfectly normal! Men," she muttered to herself. She bent closer to frown at the slowly spreading stain of scarlet against the white bandage. "I'd better take a look at this. Sit down—before you fall down," she added as she glanced up at him. He looked exhausted. Pain bracketed grooves on each side of his mouth; his eyes were reddened from lack of sleep, and his face was pale beneath the suntan and the smears of black greasepaint. "What have you been doing besides getting sliced with a knife by a man who didn't like your face?" she asked, trying to distract him as she unhooked the little metal clip from the end of the bandage and began to unwrap it from around his ribs, rerolling it as she went.

Josh drew in a deep breath and held it. Each time she reached around him to pass the roll of bandage from one hand to the other as she unwrapped it, she pressed lightly against his chest. Even as tired as he was, the rhythmic press of her body against his was a temptation he had to force himself to ignore.

"I must have torn stitches loose when I picked you up," he said, determinedly keeping his gaze fastened on the wall behind her. One look into her worried face turned up to his had been enough to tell him that there was only so much enticement he could resist. And he was damn sure she didn't mean to encourage him to make a pass. In fact, if he tried, he'd bet everything he owned that she'd slug him.

"Hmmph." She shot him a green-eyed look of reproval. "Another good reason why you shouldn't be tossing people around. I can think of several others," she added pointedly.

"Yes, ma'am, I'm sure you can." He grinned faintly. A faint gasp brought his glance away from the wall and down to her face. She was staring at his ribs, and her cheeks had lost their color, her hands clenched over the haphazardly rolled bandage. "I'll take care of it," he offered abruptly, but before he could take the bandage from her, she shook her head.

"No, I'll do it. Sit down."

This time, he obeyed her, suddenly too tired to argue. The edge of the mattress dipped as it took his weight.

"Did the doctor give you anything to put on this?" Katherine steeled herself against the surge of emotion that swept her and knelt on the floor to gently touch the edges of the angry red wound, held together with black sutures. Blood seeped from the laced-together skin. "It doesn't look like you tore out any of the stitches, but you should be resting, not throwing women around."

Her forearm brushed against his jeans-covered thigh as she leaned close to inspect the ugly gash. His skin heated with the contact. Josh grunted in acknowledgment of her last pointed comment before answering her question. "I have ointment and pain pills."

"Where's the ointment?"

"In my shirt pocket."

Katherine turned away from him and stretched to reach the shirt. The plain white tube had no printing on it and she looked from it to Josh, one tawny eyebrow lifting in inquiry. "Did the doctor give you any specific directions about using this?"

"The usual—spread it over the wound when the bandages are changed. That's about it."

"Hmm." Katherine frowned in disapproval. "Was this a real doctor you saw?"

"Yup, far as I know." Josh didn't tell her that the "doctor" had been a priest in a village even smaller than this one.

Katherine was unconvinced, but she uncapped the tube and squeezed the ointment onto her fingertips. Carefully, she spread the clear gel over the knife wound, the tip of her tongue caught between small white teeth as she concentrated.

Josh held his breath and tried to ignore the soft touch of her fingers against his bare skin.

"Well." Finished at last, Katherine drew in a deep breath and stood to stare down at him consideringly. "I suppose the doctor didn't give you any more bandages?"

"Nope—just this one. Wrap me back up, Dr. Bennington-Logan, and let's get to sleep." His nerves had had about all they could stand of her soft fingers smoothing against his hot skin, and she was so close to him that every breath he took drew in the subtle scents of perfume and woman.

"I'll do no such thing! I can't put this bandage back on you—it's not clean!"

"Lady," Josh said wearily, "right now I wouldn't

care if it was one of Miguel's bar towels. Just wrap me up and get in bed.''

Katherine shook her head. ''No, I'm not putting this bandage back on you. But one of Miguel's bar towels might work as a substitute. I'll be right back.'' She spun on her heel, but, weary as Josh was, he moved swiftly, catching her forearm in a steel-hard grip to stop her.

It halted her abruptly in midstride, and she turned back to face him with confusion written across her expressive features.

''Forget it,'' he said brusquely. ''You're not going anywhere.''

''But it won't take but a few minutes. I'm sure he won't mind.''

''No, you're not leaving this room without me— and I'm not leaving this room till tomorrow morning.''

Katherine's eyes narrowed over his face. It had taken on that implacable, dangerous look once again. Still, she would have argued with him if it hadn't been for the fatigue visible beneath his threatening glare.

''Very well,'' she conceded and his grip slackened, his fingers sliding away from her arm. ''But I am *not* putting that stained bandage on you.'' She bent and lifted the hem of her skirt.

Josh was treated to a view of well-shaped calves and knees beneath her slip. Made of yards of white cotton, flounced and full and trimmed with a wide band of lace, it covered her almost to her knees.

Katherine caught the hem's French Alençon lace in a firm grip and ruthlessly ripped it from the fine cotton, dropping it on the bare wooden floor without a care for its destruction. She tugged at a side seam of the slip until it gave way, the stitching tearing loose to leave the slip split up one side to her thigh.

Josh watched in fascination for several seconds before he could find his voice. "Just what the hell are you doing?"

Katherine looked up and caught the flash of heat in his blue gaze fastened on her legs. Suddenly self-conscious, she turned her back to him.

"I'm tearing off a strip of my slip for a bandage." She hoped her voice didn't reflect the tremors that had shivered through her in reaction to the hot awareness in his blue eyes. "Don't you ever watch John Wayne Western movies? The heroine always rips up her underskirt to bandage the wounded hero."

Interest lit Josh's eyes. "You watch John Wayne movies?"

"Yes." She looked over her shoulder at him. "I'm crazy about John Wayne. Isn't everyone?"

"Well, actually, most women I know are more interested in current movie stars."

"Hmmph." Katherine turned to face him, her skirt falling to swirl around her knees. "If most women really knew those actors they sigh over on the screen, they'd change their minds." An image of Bradley Stephens' handsome, smiling face flashed quickly to mind, and she frowned.

"Well, I suppose most women don't get the chance to actually meet actors in person," Josh offered, wondering what memory had brought that fierce frown to her face.

"No, you're probably right," she conceded. For a brief moment, silence reigned while she folded the strip of cotton torn from her slip into a thick pad.

Carefully aligning it over the angry red wound with its neat black stitches, she picked up his hand and pressed the flat of his palm against the pad. "There. Hold that in place while I wrap the bandage around you."

Josh complied, and suffered in silence while she reversed the earlier process with the bandage, wrapping it around his ribs. Once again, her breasts pressed against his chest as she reached around him. Once again, the clean scent of shampoo mingled with perfume teased his nostrils as his chin almost touched the crown of her bent head.

"There." Katherine hooked the little metal clips on the bandage end and rested back on her heels to survey with satisfaction the strips of white bandage wrapped neatly around his lower chest. "That should do it."

"Thanks," he growled reluctantly. His wound did feel better, but her ministrations had started aches in other parts of his body. He watched as she got to her feet and turned away to replace the ointment in his shirt pocket.

The air in the room was suddenly too close. Katherine felt movement behind her and heard the bedsprings squeak when he stood. She tensed, her fingers ceasing their unnecessary straightening and smoothing of his shirt against the bedpost. She glanced over her shoulder to find him turned away from her, his broad shoulders blocking the lamplight, and she noticed a twist in the bandage below his shoulder blade. She moved to smooth out the twisted linen, but before her fingers reached him, he turned toward her. The lamplight glinted off the gun he held in his right hand and she gasped, her eyes rounding with sudden fear as her gaze flew from the blue-barreled revolver to his face. She took a small, instinctive step back and away from him.

Josh read the quick fear in her green eyes and waved a hand toward the empty holster on the nightstand. "I always sleep with my gun under my pillow when I'm away from home," he said quietly, his gaze fastened unwaveringly on hers. "I feel safer."

"Oh."

He watched the fear fade from the green depths, only to be replaced with wary caution as her gaze slid away from his and flicked to the bed before returning to meet his once again. He wished there were something he could do to reassure her that she was safe, but he knew words wouldn't work. She probably wouldn't believe that he'd keep his promise until she woke up tomorrow morning and realized that she hadn't had to fight him off during the night.

He glanced at the bed and reached down to toss the blankets back.

"Climb in."

"I'll sleep on top of the blankets," Katherine said, stubbornly holding her ground.

"No," he said evenly. "*You'll* sleep under the sheet, I'll sleep on top of the sheet, and we'll both sleep under the blankets. It gets too cold in the desert to sleep without blankets."

Katherine looked at him consideringly for one long moment. His unwavering stare was unflinching and implacable.

"Very well." She bent to slip off her sandals and gathered her skirt in both hands before she knelt on the sheet-covered mattress and walked on her knees to the far side. She lay down, unconsciously holding her breath and stiffening her muscles, exhaling with silent relief when he pulled the sheet up to her chin and climbed into bed, drawing the blankets up to cover them both before turning off the lamp.

His weight on top of the sheet tugged it tightly across her body and she wiggled experimentally in an attempt to loosen it.

"Stop fidgeting," Josh growled, exhaustion pulling at him and being defeated by her movements.

"The sheet's choking me," she said, tugging at it. But it was tucked tightly under the mattress edge where the bed was pushed against the wall and it wouldn't pull free.

Josh bit off an oath and rose on his elbows. He leaned over her, his bare chest pressing her into the mattress as he caught the sheet in impatient fingers and yanked it free.

For a brief moment, Katherine felt the long length of his body press against hers. Warm and hard, it sent alarm bells jangling across her nerves and her heart raced, its quickened thuds echoing loudly in her ears.

"There." Josh shifted away from the enticing soft curves of her body and back to his own half of the bed, turning away from her to shut her out of his sight. "Now go to sleep."

She didn't respond, and within seconds he was asleep, his chest rising and falling in rhythmic breathing, one hand tucked beneath his pillow, his fingers closed around the butt of his revolver.

Katherine lay awake, staring at the ceiling where moonlight threw flickering shadows. Muted noise from the cantina below disturbed the silence; someone was playing a guitar and sporadic bursts of laughter interrupted its strummed chords.

Last night she'd had dinner at a four-star restaurant with her father and his handpicked production team that had protected, adored, and teased her on her summer visits ever since her parents' friendly divorce when she was five. She'd been in Mexico a week this time, surrounded by her surrogate family; she'd given little thought to the fact that she was in a foreign and possibly dangerous country.

She turned her head, her cheek moving against the faintly rough texture of the pillowcase. The bed in her hotel was soft and comfortable, covered with smooth sheets, plush blankets, and a silky spread. She curled her fingers over the edge of the blanket tucked beneath her chin, testing its rough, scratchy texture.

If life had been too dull lately, if each day had seemed to be a drab repeat of the day before, she'd certainly broken the habitual routine, she thought with a small, wry smile. Had it been only two weeks ago that she'd fended off another discreetly probing inquiry from her mother about marriage, complaining that there were no interesting men in her life? That all the men she knew were complacent and unremittingly dull and staid?

She stared at the blanket-draped outline of the man lying beside her, his head a dark shape against the white pillowcase in the moonlit room, his shoulders broad as he sprawled beneath the blanket. *Dull? Staid? I think I've met someone who doesn't fit the mold.* Katherine wondered with amusement what her mother would say if she knew that her only daughter was sharing a bed with a stranger in a tiny room above a rowdy cantina in an unnamed village in the Mexican interior? *Probably have a heart attack*, Katherine conceded wryly. *Now, Great-Aunt Adelaide would approve of him. Especially if she knew that he seems to be every bit as stubborn as I am. She's always said I needed a real man—whatever she means by that.* Katherine had always suspected that her great-aunt thought all real men were muscled and tough, and were secure enough in their own masculinity not to feel threatened by a woman who was strong-willed and intelligent—which was a good description of Great-Aunt Adelaide, she thought.

She lay awake a long time, listening to the even breathing of the silent man beside her and watching the patterns of moonlight and shadow flickering across the surface of the ceiling. It wasn't until the predawn hours that exhaustion finally claimed her and her drooping eyes drifted shut.

Josh shifted and tensed, his closed eyelids flickering. Something soft and silky brushed with a light, feathery touch across his chin and upper lip, and his nose twitched in reaction, his nostrils drawing in the subtle fragrance of shampoo. A smile curved his lips as he registered the feel of the unmistakably feminine face snuggled against his throat. Warm breath puffed gently against his collarbone.

Uhmm, nice. His eyes still closed, he tightened his arms around the female form lying against him, savoring with sleepy pleasure the feel of soft breasts pressed against his chest and the warmth of a slender thigh snugged between his own. Her knee nudged his inner thigh muscles just inches below his jeans zipper. His hand traveled in a slow, exploring sweep down the curve of her back and hip to catch the bend of her knee and pull it higher, and paused.

He frowned. There was something wrong here. His fingers explored and tested the textures—she was wearing clothes, and something was wrapped around her. Josh forced his heavy eyelids open and stared uncomprehendingly at the tumbled mane of silky blond hair tucked beneath his chin.

What the hell? He blinked, squeezed his eyes closed, and opened them again. The blond hair was still there. Experimentally, he tightened his arms. The press of soft curves against his own body's harder angles and planes eliminated any lingering doubt. This wasn't a dream. There really was a woman in bed with him. She wasn't just sharing his bed, she was draped across his chest and snuggled so close they were practically breathing in unison. And judging by the shade of buttery-yellow hair tickling his chin and trailing across the bare skin of his shoulder and chest, that woman was the very proper Katherine Adelaide Bennington-Logan III.

Josh stifled a groan. Contrary to his family's belief, Josh did not have a never-ending parade of girlfriends, nor did he have a girl in every port. In fact, he rarely spent enough time in any one place to develop the kind of relationship that involved waking up in the morning with a woman in his arms.

As the events of yesterday forced his sluggish mind to go from sleepiness to full awareness, Josh restrained another groan. Why had he married her? Not that it wasn't a good idea to present his mother with a bride so that he could relax and enjoy his next trip home, but actually getting married was a little extreme, even for him. If only he hadn't gone so long without sleep, maybe he would have been less impatient, less reckless.

Oh, well, he reflected philosophically. *There's nothing I can do about it now. I wonder how long it takes to get a divorce in Mexico.*

Katherine sighed and burrowed closer in her sleep, and the movement of her soft feminine curves against him felt so good he had to force himself not to respond. He vaguely remembered reassuring her the day before that their relationship would be platonic, but certain parts of his body were demanding that he forget that ridiculous promise immediately.

If I'm going to keep my word, I'd better remove myself from temptation, he admitted silently, reluctantly, to himself. *Before my natural inclination to make love to her overwhelms my good sense.* Carefully, he unwound her arms and gently eased her away from him and onto the mattress. She murmured and stirred, but didn't waken, and he heaved a sigh of relief, tinged with regret, when she was no longer snuggled against him.

He tossed back the blankets and carefully left the bed. Katherine slumbered on, unaware of his struggle with his conscience while he stood beside the bed, staring down at her. Her shoulder-length blond hair had worked its way free of the pins that held it, and tumbled around her face in a silken fall. Relaxed with sleep, her face had lost its haughty reserve and was innocently vulnerable, the soft curve of her mouth bare of lipstick, her thick lashes creating golden-brown fans below closed lids. Josh wrenched his fascinated gaze away from her blanket-draped form and went to the washstand.

Katherine woke all at once, her lashes lifting to

reveal sleepy green eyes. She frowned at the rough cotton pillowcase beneath her cheek while her mind scrambled to make sense of her unfamiliar surroundings. The sound of water splashing distracted her and she pushed her hair out of her eyes with one hand while she levered herself upward, bracing a forearm against the sheet-covered mattress for support. She searched the sparsely furnished room, and her gaze widened when it encountered the broad, naked back of a man. He bent forward over the washstand, splashing water over his face repeatedly before he straightened, his hands groping for the towel that hung over a bar attached to the stand. His face disappeared in the folds of cotton toweling and with unblinking fascination she watched the ripple and flex of muscles across his biceps and shoulders while he dried his face.

Josh lowered the towel and glanced over his shoulder at the bed. He stared into green eyes wide with bewildered confusion. *Uh-oh*. He waited patiently without speaking and slowly, realization dawned in the emerald depths and her confusion was replaced with a wary reserve.

"Good morning." His voice was carefully neutral and reflected none of the mixed feelings that warred within him.

"Good morning." Her normally husky voice was even more so with sleep. "Why didn't you wake me?"

"I only just woke up myself." Josh turned away and slung the towel back over the bar.

Katherine looked at the shaft of warm sunshine that threw a long golden bar of light across the floor. "What time is it?"

Josh glanced at the face of the utilitarian watch strapped to his wrist. "Nearly six o'clock. Time to get moving—I want to be in Santa Rosa and on a plane out of Mexico long before noon."

"All right, fine," Katherine answered automatically, her sluggish senses struggling to keep up with him. She wasn't a person who bounced out of bed in the morning, bright-eyed and bushy-tailed. She needed a cup of coffee and at least thirty minutes of unbroken silence for her brain to gear up to functional level.

She shoved back the sheet and blankets and sat up, swinging her legs over the edge of the bed. Her toes curled in protest when her feet touched the cool floor, but the temperature outside was already climbing and the air in the room was keeping pace. She yawned delicately and stretched, urging her sluggish brain to wake up.

Josh hid a grin. She reminded him of a sleek little cat, stretching and blinking in the early morning sunlight.

"I'll leave you alone to use the facilities, such as they are." He waved a hand toward the washstand before catching his rumpled khaki shirt up from the bedpost. He shrugged into the shirt and buttoned it with quick, deft movements before dropping down onto the mattress beside her and bending to tug on his boots. Katherine didn't say a word. She just sat there with her hands folded in her lap, watching him with owl-like intensity. He looked sideways at her and a little frown pulled down his brows and narrowed his eyes. "You're sure you're all right?"

She blinked once, twice, and irritation flickered in her eyes. "Of course I'm all right." A slender hand lifted to hide another yawn. "It just takes me a few minutes to wake up."

Josh couldn't help it. A smile broke over his face, transforming the stern, almost harsh lines into striking handsomeness. "Okay, sweetheart, if you say so." He reached up and ruffled her hair in an instinctive gesture of friendliness.

He caught her in a weak moment. Men did *not* touch her with such familiarity, except her father. But before she could think of a scathing rebuff, Josh had stood, slung his holster and gun over his shoulder, and crossed to the door. He paused halfway over the threshold to smile at her.

"I'll order us some coffee and breakfast—hurry up."

"Yes, master," she managed to mutter, several moments after the door had closed on his broad back. She stood up and walked across the cool floor to the washstand with its mirror. "Oh, yuk!" she groaned, wincing at her reflection. Her hair fell in a thick, rumpled mane to her shoulders, her eyes were heavy-lidded and sleepy, and her face was completely bare of makeup. She looked down and groaned again at the wrinkles that sleep had pressed into her skirt. Her bare toes caught her attention and she looked around the room until she found her shoes, sitting neatly side by side on the floor beneath the bed. She felt a little better after the sandals were on her feet, as if she were a little more prepared to meet the world, and by the time she'd washed with cold water and smoothed the tangles from her hair with the comb Josh had left for her, she was starting to approach normal.

Walking down the stairs, she ran her tongue experimentally over her teeth. *Brushing one's teeth with a corner of a washcloth and cold water leaves something to be desired*, she decided. *But still, I'm proud of myself for being so inventive.*

The cantina was nearly empty. Katherine paused on the bottom step to search the room for Josh and found him seated at a table against the back wall. He was sipping from a thick mug, and the irresistible aroma of coffee drew Katherine away from the stairs and across the room to him.

"Buenos días, señora," Miguel called from behind the bar.

Katherine smiled vaguely in his general direction but never swerved from her goal.

Josh didn't miss her fixation on the pot of coffee, and as she slid into the chair opposite him, he finished filling a cup and pushed it across the tabletop toward her. He leaned back in his chair, silently watching her. It was positively uncanny to see her sleepy eyes go from somnolence to bright awareness as she finished her second serving and held out her cup for more.

"How long will it take us to drive to Santa Rosa?" she asked, leaning back in her chair as Rosa placed a plate of scrambled eggs and beans in front of her.

"Not quite two hours." Josh spooned hot sauce from a pottery bowl over his eggs and beans.

Katherine restrained a shudder at the amount of hot sauce he used and watched incredulously as he took a bite and swallowed without so much as a grimace. He glanced up and nudged the bowl of green chile salsa toward her.

"No—thank you." She took a small, testing bite of the eggs and sighed with relief to find that they didn't make her breathe fire. In fact, they were quite good. It wasn't until her plate was clean and she sat cradling a mug of coffee in both hands that she returned to her original question. "So I'll be back at my hotel in less than two hours?"

"Yes."

"And then what?"

"Then we catch a plane for the States."

"Where in the States?"

"Minneapolis."

"Minneapolis?" Intrigued, Katherine returned her cup to the tabletop and leaned forward, resting her forearms on the table. "I've never been to Minneapolis—why are we going there?"

"Because it's the closest airport to our destination."

Katherine lifted a brow and gave him a skeptical, long-suffering look. "Are we going to play Twenty Questions? Or are you going to tell me where we're really going?"

Josh shifted uncomfortably in his chair and fixed her with a moody stare. He was reluctant to confess that he'd insisted on marriage partly because she'd irritated the hell out of him. In retrospect, it had been a crazy idea, but now that he was already married to her, he had nothing to lose. He might as well go through with it.

"I'll tell you before we get there," he said.

"Why can't you tell me now?"

He didn't answer her. Instead, he took a pair of dark glasses from his shirt pocket and slid them on his nose, effectively concealing his expression. He stood, pausing for a moment to stare down at her. "Because you don't need to know yet."

Before she could protest, he was striding away from her toward the door letting out onto the street.

"Finish your coffee—you won't get any more until we reach Santa Rosa," he said over his shoulder.

"But wait! Where are you going?" Katherine half rose from her chair but she was too late. He'd already disappeared through the doorway. For a moment, she considered racing after him. But then she thought better of it and shrugged, dropping back down into her seat. *If he didn't desert me yesterday, he's not likely to go off and leave me now,* she decided, and poured another cup of coffee.

The jeep rattled and shook as it bounced through yet another chuckhole in the road. Katherine clutched the edge of the ripped leather seat cushion with one hand and the windowless doorframe with the other. She'd long since braided her hair to keep it from flying in her face as the hot wind generated by their passing whipped through the glassless windows of the battered jeep. She was hot, dusty, and her teeth felt as if they'd been permanently rattled loose from her jaw, but she felt exhilarated by the wild ride. Josh had driven through wild country on a road that was little more than a desert track. They'd raced across sandy, cactus-dotted flats and climbed rocky mountains, and Katherine had felt her heart leap into her throat a dozen times as the jeep had followed narrow tracks around the edges of cliffs with the agility of a mountain goat.

"How much farther?" She had to shout to make herself heard.

Josh glanced sideways at her. Her cheeks were

flushed with heat, and perspiration beaded her upper lip and glistened in the hollow of her throat. The braid she'd wound her hair into kept most of the blond mane out of her eyes, but tendrils had escaped and the wind whipped them around her face. Her eyes glittered with excitement and a smile of pure, reckless enjoyment curved her mouth.

"Not much longer—maybe another half hour."

"Oh. That's too bad."

She sounded disappointed. Josh shot her another glance and found her smile had disappeared, the excitement dimmed in her green eyes.

"If I didn't know better," he drawled, "I'd swear you're enjoying this."

FOUR

"I *am* enjoying this," she informed him.

"It's not the sort of thing I thought you would like," he commented, his attention back on the track that stretched ahead of them. He downshifted and braked with casual, practiced confidence, and the jeep slid sideways around a curve and climbed out of a dry wash. When he looked back at her, she was laughing, her eyes gleaming with reckless joy once again. "I can see you appreciate the finer points of wrestling a jeep through the desert."

"I love it! Where did you learn to drive like this?" Katherine hadn't missed the easy way he handled the jeep, shifting, braking, and steering with an expert coordination that made her wonder if he'd ever driven race cars.

"From my brother," Josh replied, slowing to a stop as the track they were following reached an intersection with a paved highway. He glanced both ways before pulling out onto the blacktop and accelerating, going through the gears with a swift efficiency.

"Your brother?" Katherine relaxed her death grip on the seat and brushed the hair out of her eyes. "Where did he learn to drive?"

"The Daytona 500." Josh shot her stunned features a quick look and chuckled with amusement. "There's Santa Rosa." He pointed out the dust-streaked windshield at the city shimmering in the heat haze ahead of them. "What hotel are you staying in?"

"You could have been more polite to my father," Katherine said for the sixth time in as many hours. She turned away from the jet airliner's window and frowned in disapproval at the man lounging in the blue-upholstered seat beside her. Dressed in a clean khaki shirt that was a duplicate of the ripped, stained one he'd discarded earlier, a clean pair of tight faded jeans, and gray cowboy boots, he was as uncommunicative as ever.

"Yup," Josh grunted, his eyes closed. His arms were folded across his chest, his long legs stretched out as far as possible in the cramped space between their seats and the row ahead of them. He was trying to catch up on missed sleep, but was having little luck.

It was perfectly clear to Katherine that he didn't want to discuss the issue, but she did. "You could at least have let me explain."

Josh opened one eye and looked at her. "Why?"

"Because he was worried, that's why! It's not exactly an everyday occurrence for me to sail into his office and tell him I'm married and I'm leaving on my honeymoon! You barely took time to say hello and shake his hand before you said good-bye and hustled me off!''

Josh shrugged, closed his eye, and settled deeper into his seat. ''He would have been a lot more worried if he knew the real circumstances. He's better off not knowing anything outside the fact that we're married. I suppose you think I should have chatted longer with your mother, too?''

''No, we can telephone her again when we get to wherever it is we're going . . .''

''Good afternoon.'' The captain's deep voice came over the intercom and interrupted Katherine. ''We are now approaching Minneapolis–St. Paul International Airport. Please return your seats to an upright position and fasten your seat belts. Thank you.''

The ensuing flurry of activity of landing and deplaning prevented her from pursuing the subject further, and within a half hour, Katherine was following Josh across the terminal to a counter marked ''Connors Air Freight.'' He dropped Katherine's three bags on the floor alongside his own small duffel bag and glanced around the vacant counter before ringing the customer-service bell.

Katherine set the cosmetics case she carried down on the floor next to the other bags. ''Are we flying somewhere on a freight carrier?'' she asked, her curious gaze taking in the utilitarian appearance of the Connors counter.

''Nope,'' Josh replied, ringing the bell again.

''Then what are we doing here?''

''The owner is a friend of mine,'' he said. ''I

leave my—vehicle with him when I fly out of Minneapolis.''

"Oh.''

"Joshua!'' a deep male voice boomed in welcome, and Katherine looked up to see a bear of a man, in a blue coverall with "Connors Air Freight'' stitched in white over his pocket, walk through the doorway behind the counter. He leaned over the counter and caught Josh's hand in one big paw. "How you been, son? Long time no see.''

"How are you, Bill?'' Josh returned the handshake with feeling, a wide grin splitting his face.

"Fine, fine. Your brother Trace was up here to pick up some parts for a '38 coupe last week and told me to expect you sometime soon.''

"Oh, yeah? Any news from home?''

"Just that Cole's getting married—but I expect you already know that. Isn't that why you're home?''

"Yeah, that's why.''

Katherine listened with fascination, her head swiveling from one man to the other as if watching a tennis match. She'd learned more about Josh in his few minutes of conversation with Bill than she'd managed to wring out of him all day.

"I stopped to get my keys and find out if you've got room to take our luggage on a flight out to the Spirit Lake airport tonight.''

"Sure.'' Bill pulled open a drawer beneath the counter and extracted a set of keys. "Got your keys right here—and Steve's heading south about seven o'clock, he'll be glad to drop off your bags.'' The big man dropped the keys into Josh's outstretched palm and turned inquisitive, friendly blue eyes on Katherine. "I don't think I've met your lady, Josh.''

Josh had known this moment would come. Should he introduce Katherine to Bill as his wife? If he did, Bill would be on the telephone the minute they walked away from the counter, and everyone in CastleRock would know he was married before he crossed the Iowa state line. He decided on a neutral course.

"This is Katherine, Bill. Katherine, this is an old friend of mine from CastleRock, Bill Middleton."

"How do you do, Mr. Middleton. I'm very pleased to meet you."

Bill grinned at the polite words and his ham-size hand enveloped her graciously extended fingers. "I'm pleased to meet you, too, Katherine." He released her hand and winked broadly at Josh. "Your taste is as good as Trace's, Josh. She's mighty pretty."

"Thanks, Bill," Josh said dryly. He could see the question in Katherine's eyes and before she could voice it, he spoke again. "And thanks for delivering our luggage." He caught Katherine's waist and moved her away from the counter.

"Tell your folks hello for me," Bill called after them, and Josh lifted a hand in acknowledgment.

Katherine was half running, trying to keep up with his long strides. He didn't slow down until they exited a side door of the terminal.

"How many brothers do you have?" she asked, her low heels clicking quickly across the tarmac as they walked toward a hangar with "Connors Air Freight" painted in huge block letters over the cavernous opening. The late afternoon sun still held all the heat of an August summer day and she narrowed her eyes against its glare.

"Two." He stopped her just outside the hangar. "Wait here. I'll be right out."

"But—" It was no use. He was already walking away from her, and quickly disappeared inside the hangar. *I wonder if that man ever carries on a normal conversation!* she fumed silently. She had the definite impression that he was hiding something. Every time she asked him a question that even remotely came close to being personal, he either pretended to be asleep or walked away from her.

A small Cessna landed on the runway behind her and she turned to watch as it taxied to a halt. It was a good three city blocks away, but the noise it made distracted her. The engine sound died away and the doors opened to let a family of five clamber down to the tarmac. Katherine watched the children jump to the ground with pent-up exuberance, and wondered idly how long they'd been cooped up in the small plane.

"Are you ready to go?"

Josh's voice startled her and she turned quickly to face him, going abruptly still when she saw what he sat on.

The motorcycle he straddled was a gleaming, customized, chrome-and-black-lacquer work of art. Katherine's green eyes widened as her gaze moved slowly over the chopped bike, but narrowed with suspicion when she looked at Josh. She couldn't see his expression behind the dark lenses of his sunglasses, but the whole line of his body as he sat on the bike, one booted foot planted securely on the pavement to keep the bike upright, told her quite clearly that he fully expected her to pitch a fit.

Her glance flicked from his face to the chrome

wheels of the '63 Harley-Davidson. She had the feeling this was some sort of test, but she had no idea what the questions were. *Oh, well.* She shrugged mentally. *At the very least, I'll have a new experience to share with Aunt Adelaide.*

Josh watched in confusion as she slipped the strap of her small purse over her head, settling the leather envelope against the opposite hip. Then she bent over and caught the hem at the back of her calf-length green skirt, pulling it between her knees and upward until she could tuck it into the waistband. It turned the voluminous silk skirt into harem pants. Sexy harem pants, he reflected as he stared at her knees and the strip of bare thigh visible.

"Is that my helmet?" Katherine asked calmly, pointing at the black headgear that hung over the short chrome cheater bar at the end of the leather seat.

"Yeah." Josh twisted to take the helmet off the bar and beckoned Katherine closer. "Let's see if it fits." Carefully, he settled the helmet over her head and tightened the strap under her chin. When Katherine would have stepped away, he stayed her with a hand at her nape.

"What?" she asked, too aware of his jeans-covered thigh against her bare knee and the warmth of his hand against her skin.

Josh wanted to pull her closer and kiss her. He'd been fighting the almost overpowering urge to do so ever since he'd awakened this morning to find her snuggled against him in bed. For a long moment, his need to pull her closer warred with his promise to keep their relationship platonic. Finally, honor won, and he released her.

"It's a good thing you're wearing a long-sleeved shirt," he said, his voice rasping. He flicked her green silk sleeve with a forefinger. "Otherwise, you'd get a windburn. Have you got sunscreen for your face?"

"Yes." She fumbled in her purse with trembling fingers, grateful for the distraction, until she found a small tube. "I bought it for Mexico."

"Better put it on," he ordered brusquely, and watched while she smoothed the cream over her face and throat, noticing once again what beautiful, kiss-able skin she had. With an effort, he forced his mind away from thoughts of kissing her and, with a hand on her shoulder, gently moved her back and away from the bike. He kick-started the engine and throt-tled it for several moments to keep it running, the staccato roar deafening, before he bent sideways and lowered the footpegs on each side. "All right," he said to Katherine, reading the nervousness in her stiff shoulders. Would she really go through with it? "Climb aboard."

Katherine complied, her hands gingerly clasping his shoulders as she swung a leg over the leather seat and sat down, immediately removing her hands.

"Hang on," he said over the engine noise, and the big bike moved forward.

The smooth surge of power sent Katherine sliding back against the cheater bar and she gasped, lurching forward to grab fistfuls of Josh's shirt at his waist.

Josh hid a grin. He was going to enjoy this. The bike wove its way slowly through the parking lot, and when they left the lot to move into traffic, he purposely let out the clutch and gave the bike more throttle than he needed. Katherine's grip tightened even more and his smile widened.

The street curved to the right and Josh automatically leaned the bike into the turn. He was forcibly reminded that he'd forgotten to warn Katherine of one of the basic principles of motorcycle riding when she instinctively leaned away from him to the left. When the street straightened, he slowed.

"When I lean the bike into a turn, go with me," he yelled over his shoulder.

"What?" Katherine couldn't hear him, so she erased the scant half inch she was scrupulously keeping between her breasts and his broad back and leaned forward until her face was only inches from his.

"I said, lean into the turns with me." He kept one eye on the infrequent traffic on the road while he talked. "If you try to stay upright while we're going around a curve, you're fighting the bike and me."

"Oh." Katherine considered that for a moment. It sounded dangerous, but he handled the bike as if they were old friends, and since this was her first experience, it made sense to listen to him. "All right," she yelled in his ear.

"Good." He nodded with satisfaction. "And wrap your arms around my waist. I feel like I'm going to lose you every time I take off from a stop sign."

"All right, all right!" she grumbled, and forced her fists to unwind from his shirt so she could slide her arms around his waist. By necessity, the move tucked her against him, but she had to admit, she felt more secure.

By the time they left the Minneapolis–St. Paul suburbs behind and caught the narrow highway south toward the Iowa line, she'd lost her fear and was thoroughly enjoying the ride. It was a beautiful summer day. Puffy white cotton clouds floated in the deep blue sky and the sun smiled down on them. The wind stirred by their passing billowed their shirts around their bodies.

Josh had a lot of time to think on the trip south. He almost regretted tricking Katherine in Mexico. She was being such a good sport about the unorthodox methods of transportation he'd subjected her to that he was beginning to doubt his first opinion of her as a spoiled little rich girl.

No, he corrected himself. *She's definitely rich. I'm just not so sure how spoiled she is.* Sharing a platonic bed with her in Mexico had been tough, even though he'd been nearly comatose with exhaustion at the time. *Well, I'm not comatose now*, he thought with a groan. *We're married, I'm her husband, and not touching her is driving me crazy!*

There was something about taking vows, whether you meant them or not, he decided, that set off an irrational possessiveness in a man. He knew very well that this marriage was temporary and pretend, yet a part of his brain urged him to claim all the rights he was entitled to as a husband. *Not to mention the way my body feels about being her husband*, he thought wryly, registering the warmth of her hands against his midriff.

On the heels of that thought came another. He still hadn't old her where they were going. Or why.

Oh, damn, he thought with reluctance. He couldn't put it off any longer; they'd long since crossed the Minnesota border into Iowa, and in another half hour they'd be in CastleRock. He slowed the bike and pulled into the gravel parking lot of a gas station/ market just off the highway.

It wasn't until he'd bought two cans of icy-cold soda and seated Katherine on the wooden bench of a picnic table under an old oak tree beside the market that he was ready to tell her why they'd stopped.

Katherine sipped her soda and glanced sideways at Josh. He sat beside her, his long legs stretched out in front of him and crossed at the ankles. His arms were propped on the tabletop at his back, his can of soda dangling from the fingers of one hand. He stared moodily at the Harley, leaning on its kick-stand a few feet away. It was clear he was trying to find the words to tell her something, but she was damned if she'd make it easy for him. Not after he'd refused to answer questions. So she silently sipped her soda, tipping her head back to swing her hair loose down her back and reveling in the breeze that rippled through it. The helmet made her feel pro-tected, but it was warm inside, and her scalp was damp beneath her thick mane of hair.

"I think it's time you know where we're going," he said finally, slanting a glance at her from behind the protection of his dark lenses. She didn't say any-thing; she only looked at him, waiting without speak-ing. He shoved his fingers through his wind-ruffled hair. "CastleRock. It's my hometown—my family still lives there. That's why I wanted a wife—be-cause of my family. And weddings."

He wasn't making a lot of sense. Katherine waited patiently, silently eyeing him, inwardly enjoying his obvious discomfort.

Josh sighed and started over. "I have two brothers and a sister. In the last couple of years, they've all decided to get married. First there was my little sister, Sarah—she married Jesse, a friend of my older brother Trace. Then Trace got married—to Lily. And next week my oldest brother, Cole, is getting married, to a lady named Melanie. For some odd reason, Sarah's marriage triggered an obsession with weddings with my mother. She's a normally well-adjusted, reasonable woman, but she's decided that she wants all of us married and settled down in CastleRock. Every time I go home, she bugs me about getting married from the minute I walk through the front door until the minute I leave. It drives me crazy." He paused and glanced sideways at her silent figure once again. "I decided in Mexico that the only way to enjoy Cole's wedding was to show up with a wife of my own. That's where you come in."

Katherine stared at him, disbelief written across her face. "Are you telling me that the reason you wanted a wife is so your mother won't harass you about getting married?"

"It sounds pretty lame, doesn't it? But yeah," he said with a self-deprecating grin, "that's about it."

A smile twitched the corners of Katherine's mouth, worked its way into a wide grin, and was replaced with laughter that bubbled up and soon had her weak with giggles.

"I thought you were up to something exciting and maybe dangerous," she finally got out when she could speak. "And all the time you just wanted to fool your mother?"

"You've never met my mother, or you wouldn't be laughing," Josh muttered, a red flush of embarrassment streaking his cheeks. "She can be relentless."

"Actually . . ." Katherine wiped tears of laughter from her eyes and gave him a considering look, a grin still tugging at her lips. "It's not a very admirable act—deceiving your mother."

"Yeah, well," he said, his glance chasing away from hers, "I wasn't exactly myself the day we met, and besides, I never said I was a nice guy."

"Oh, I don't know about that." She gave him a sidelong, mischievous smile that had his temperature skyrocketing. "I think you're sweet."

"Sweet?" He stared at the dazzling smile that curved her mouth and lit her features with warm, friendly approval. He wasn't sure he wanted her to think he was sweet.

"Yes, sweet," she repeated, and in an impulsive move she leaned sideways and planted a quick kiss on his cheek.

He stiffened, his fingers clenching around the aluminum soda can with punishing force. The warm brush of her lips against his cheek was sweet torture. He looked down at her face, softened with affection, and knew he should say something crude to make her dislike him and return them to being adversaries, but he couldn't bring himself to do it.

"So." He cleared his throat and smiled hopefully back at her. "Does that mean you're willing to declare a truce and help me get through this?"

Katherine considered his offer. She'd given her word and she wouldn't back out, but it would be easier if they were a team.

"Will you stop walking away from me when I ask you questions?" she asked gravely.

Josh nodded. "Yes."

"Will you answer my questions?"

"If I can—as long as you don't ask about my work."

"Why? What do you do?"

"I work for the Department of Immigration," he answered, meeting her gaze with a level stare. "But most of what I do is confidential and I can't talk about it—not to anyone."

Katherine believed him, so after a moment's consideration, she set her can of soda between them on the bench and reached out. "All right—you have a deal, Mr. McFadden. A truce."

Josh grinned and closed her fingers in his. Chilled from the cold soda, they warmed quickly in his callused palm. "We have a truce, that means we're partners, Mrs. McFadden."

Katherine wasn't sure she trusted the warm grin that tilted his mouth. He had a smile that could only be described as sexy, and it made her heart rate speed up and her throat go dry. *But he's not dull*, she reminded herself. *Maybe a little dangerous, but I can handle him*. She ignored the little voice that chuckled disbelievingly at her in the back of her mind.

Josh tossed his empty can into the trash barrel on the far side of the tree and stood, pulling Katherine up after him.

"Come on, Mrs. McFadden. I want you to meet your in-laws."

CastleRock was a beautiful small town. Built on the shores of a large lake, its wide, tree-shaded boulevards were peaceful and quiet under the slanting rays of the setting sun. Its sleepy quiet was broken by the muted roar of the Harley's mufflers as Josh downshifted to turn into the street where his parents lived.

Katherine stared with unabashed interest when Josh slowed to a halt at the curb in front of a gracious, well-maintained Victorian house set in the center of a wide green lawn. A huge, stately oak tree shaded one side, and roses lined the sidewalk that led to the front porch.

Josh had barely cut the engine when the front door flew open and a trio of women spilled out onto the porch, laughing and shouting greetings. Katherine stepped off the bike and unstrapped the helmet, tugging it off with relief and shaking her hair free. When she glanced back at the house, she found the three had stopped to stare at her with obvious surprise.

"Josh," she said softly to claim his attention. His head was bent as he lowered the kickstand and rested the bike on it before swinging his leg over the seat to dismount.

"Yeah." He looked up and read the quiet warning in her eyes. Her glance moved from his face to the group on the porch and his followed. He took in the lively curiosity on each face before he looked back at Katherine. "This is your last chance to back out, Kate. Are you still willing to go through with this?"

Katherine's gaze flicked from his face to the porch and back again. "Of course I am," she said calmly. "I gave you my word. Let's get on with it, Joshua."

He smiled. He liked the way she said his name.

Josh's fingers caught Katherine's in a possessive grip and he tugged her gently around the chrome-wire front wheel of the bike, over the curb and grass, and up the sidewalk toward the house.

"Hey, Mom," he called. "Aren't you even going to say hello?"

Jeannie McFadden laughed and ran lightly down the steps to catch him in a swift hug. Josh released Katherine's hand to return the hug and Katherine took a small step back. The two young women left standing on the painted porch boards smiled at her and she smiled tentatively back. The two were as different as night and day, for one had ebony hair that swung almost to her waist and lavender eyes, while the other was blond with blue eyes and bore a striking resemblance to Josh. She cradled a baby against her shoulder, its tiny head with its cap of black curls nestled into the curve of her neck.

Katherine guessed that the blonde must be Josh's sister, Sarah, and she wondered briefly if the brunette was one of his sisters-in-law.

Josh released his mother and turned to Katherine, slipping an arm around her waist with easy possessiveness to draw her forward.

"Mom, I want you to meet Katherine Bennington-Logan McFadden." He smiled down into her eyes. "We were married yesterday."

Katherine watched his mother's expression go from friendly interest to shock, her gray eyes rounding with surprise, before her mouth curved in a dazzling smile of delight.

"Married! You're married?" She threw her arms around her tall son in another quick hug before she did the same to Katherine. "Oh, my goodness! This is such a surprise! Welcome to the family!"

"Thank you." Katherine returned Jeannie's hug, relieved when Josh tugged her gently back to his side.

The two young women left the porch and added their congratulations to Jeannie's.

"I'm Sarah." The young blond woman flipped her wheat-colored braid back over her shoulder and held out her hand to shake Katherine's with warm friendliness. "And this is Jennifer." Sarah tilted her head back and turned the baby's sleepy face toward them. "Wake up, Jennie," she said softly, stroking a forefinger gently over one petal-soft cheek, "and say hello to your uncle Josh and aunt Katherine."

The baby's dark lashes lifted, revealing miniature duplicates of her mother's sapphire blue eyes, and Josh laughed with delight.

"You've got your mama's eyes, darlin'." He released Katherine and held out his arms.

Emotion twisted in Katherine as she watched his big hands tenderly cradle the tiny little girl. Jennifer lay in the crook of his arm without protest, her eyes round with fascination as she stared up into Josh's face. His finger traced the tiny, neat little shells of her ears and tested the silky swirls of fine black hair that curled over her head, before slipping into the little hand that immediately closed into a fist and trapped him.

"Hey, that's quite a grip." He grinned at Sarah. "We might have us a football player here."

Sarah laughed. "That's what Jesse says. I keep telling him that he ought to wait until she can walk before he teaches her to play touch."

"Hah," Josh crooned to the smiling baby. "Don't listen to her. We'll have you playing touch football with the big guys by the time you're two." To his delight, Jennifer blew a bubble. "See," he said triumphantly, "she agrees with me."

"She probably has gas," Sarah said dryly, and reached out to take the baby from him.

"Spoilsport," Josh growled, his blue eyes soft with warm affection as he watched Sarah settle Jennifer against her shoulder again. "What do you think, Kate?" He turned his attention back to Katherine.

Katherine was still off-balance, trying to equate the gentleness with which he handled the tiny Jennifer with the dangerous outlaw with the knife wound across his ribs.

"Kate?" She was staring at him, her green eyes soft with bemusement as they searched his. Josh slid an arm around her waist and drew her close. "Katy? Is something wrong?"

"Wrong? No." She tore her gaze from his and looked at the three women. They were eyeing her and Josh with approval and she realized that he was practically hugging her against him with familiar intimacy. She eased herself away from the warm security of his hard body. "No, nothing's wrong. I guess I'm a little tired from the trip."

"Of course you are." Jeannie waved them all ahead of her up the steps. "And here I am, keeping you standing outside." They entered the house and Jeannie paused. "My goodness, I was so excited about you two being married that I didn't introduce Lily. Katherine, this is my daughter-in-law, Lily; she's married to Josh's older brother Trace."

"Hello, Katherine." Lily smiled and took Katherine's hand in a warm clasp. "I'm delighted to meet you—welcome to the family."

"Thank you." Katherine looked closely at the lovely brunette for the first time and the familiarity of her features struck a chord. "You look so much like—are you Lily Townsend?"

"Yes, I am. Actually, I'm Lily Townsend McFadden. I added my married name to my stage name."

"Oh, my goodness," Katherine said faintly.

Lily looked from Katherine's stunned features to Josh's bland expression and quirked an ebony brow at him, her violet eyes sparkling with amusement. "You mean Josh didn't tell you? Shame on you, Joshua. What else didn't you tell her about us?"

Katherine turned to look up, her green eyes narrowing threateningly. "Yes, *Joshua*," she said sweetly. "What else didn't you tell me?"

He shrugged. "Nothing I can think of—I did mention that Mom writes mysteries, didn't I?"

"No," she said with enforced patience, "you didn't."

"Yeah, well." He grinned at her with little-boy innocence. "Mom is Jeannie McFadden—she writes mysteries—you know, the kind with bodies stuffed into trunks and the butler who doesn't do it."

Katherine's gaze switched from Josh's face to Jeannie's. "*You're* Jeannie McFadden? You wrote the Mack Montana detective series?"

The slender woman smiled and nodded, brown curls bobbing. "I'm afraid so."

"Good grief." Katherine slowly shook her head in disbelief. "Is there anything else I should know about this family?"

"Does she know about Cole?" Sarah asked Josh.

"Oh, sure," he said with nonchalant assurance.

"What about Cole?" Katherine asked ominously.

"I told you about Cole," Josh said. "Remember, I told you he learned to drive in the Daytona 500."

"Yes—so?"

Josh shifted his weight from one foot to the other and tucked his thumbs into his back pockets. "Well, actually, to tell the truth—he won the Daytona 500, several times."

"Oh." Katherine's expression spoke volumes. Although she was far too well bred to speak her thoughts aloud, the look she gave Josh left him in no doubt that she was furious with him. "Is there anything else—about anyone else?"

"Nope, I think that's about it," he said with relief. He hoped he could apologize before she started yelling.

Jeannie, Sarah, and Lily exchanged amused glances. It looked as if Josh had finally met a woman who didn't fawn over him and was perfectly capable of giving as good as she got.

"Well," Jeannie said bracingly, breaking the small silence, "why don't you take Katherine on up to your room, Josh, and you can show her where the bathroom is and where to find fresh towels. We'll be in the kitchen having coffee." She ushered Sarah and Lily ahead of her down the hall toward the kitchen, but paused to half turn back to them. "Josh, where's your luggage? I know you couldn't carry anything on that motorcycle—surely you didn't make your bride come visiting without any clothes?"

"No, Mom. We flew into Minneapolis and I had Bill Middleton send our luggage out on Connors' next flight. Our bags were probably at the airport in Spirit Lake before we got to CastleRock."

"Oh, that's all right, then." She gave Katherine a friendly, encouraging smile and hurried off down the hall.

"She's nice," Katherine murmured as she climbed the stairs, "and so are Sarah and Lily." She threw a threatening glare over her shoulder at Josh, who climbed the carpet-covered treads behind her. "But *you*, I am going to kill."

"Who, me?" They reached the top of the stairs and walked down the hallway. "What did I do?"

He stopped, turned the glass knob of a door half-way down the hall, and pushed the door inward.

"What did you do?" Katherine glared at him as she automatically stepped over the threshold and turned to face him, waiting until he'd shoved the door shut. "Not only did you *not* answer questions I asked you, but you purposely didn't tell me . . ."

She turned away from him to pace angrily into the room and halted abruptly, her voice going silent as she stared at the four-poster double bed sitting in solitary splendor in the center of the room.

FIVE

Uh-oh! I forgot about the bed! Josh stared at the comfortable maple bedstead. Jeannie had replaced the battered bunk beds from his youth with the antique bed after he'd left home. How could he have forgotten?

Katherine dragged her gaze away from the double bed and turned to stare wordlessly at him.

"I swear I forgot about the bed," he said quickly, wincing at the accusation in her green eyes. "I had bunk beds in here when I was a kid—Mom replaced them when I left."

"I am *not* sleeping with you in that bed," she said flatly. She refused to admit that she wasn't afraid of his taking advantage of her. After the long, uneventful night spent in the narrow bed in Mexico, she was convinced that she could trust his word. It was she herself Katherine didn't trust. Wide awake, she had to stifle impulses to touch him, and she was becoming far too accustomed to his touching her, holding her hand, or sliding an arm around her waist. Without her conscious self to guard her, who knew what she might do in her sleep? No, she was *definitely* not going to share a bed with him.

Josh looked at the determined, militant set of her chin and ran the fingers of one hand through his hair in distraction before sliding his hands into his jeans pocket and lifting his shoulders in a helpless male shrug. "I don't know what to tell you, honey." The endearment slipped out unnoticed. "If I tell Mom we need another bed, how am I going to explain why?"

Katherine stared at him for one long, silent moment. "You're right." She sighed. "We've only been married one day. It would look very strange to want separate beds already."

"It would look strange to my folks to want separate beds after two years, or two decades, or ever," Josh said with definite sureness.

Katherine looked unconvinced. "Well, one of us will just have to sleep on the floor." She tested the resiliency of the braided rug with the toe of one shoe. "At least we have a rug."

"Hmm," Josh grunted noncommitally. He didn't plan for either of them to sleep anywhere except in the bed, but he decided to remain silent. He'd wait until bedtime before the inevitable argument. "I'll show you where the bathroom is before we head back downstairs."

"I like your family." Katherine slipped her blouse onto a hanger and hung it in the closet next to Josh's shirts and slacks. She ignored the intimacy of her skirt and blouse hanging next to his clothing and closed the white enameled door. "They're nice."

"Think so?" Josh gave her a lopsided grin.

"I know so." She laughed at the expression of doubt on his face and tucked her hands into the pockets of the robe she wore. It was Josh's, and the blue, wraparound terry cloth that was probably knee-length on him reached to midcalf on her, the shoulder seams hitting her halfway to her elbows. "And you know it, too. You just won't admit it."

"Hmm," he growled and turned his back on her to empty his pockets onto the bureau.

He wasn't a man who readily admitted to being sentimental, she thought with an inward smile. She was beginning to suspect that his tough exterior hid a heart that was marshmallow-soft where his family was concerned.

Her glance moved past him and traveled over the lamplit bedroom that enclosed them in intimacy. Outside the tall, lace-curtained, old-fashioned window, crickets chirped and moths fluttered against the screen in the warm darkness of the night. Inside, the lamp on the bedside table threw shadows across the wall and gleamed with gold light over the bed with its folded-back sheets and soft pillows.

Josh turned away from the bureau and began to unbutton his shirt, pausing as he glanced up to find Katherine's gaze fastened on the inviting coziness of the bed. Unnoticed by her, he studied the little worried frown that furrowed her brow.

"I'm sorry Connors Air didn't get our bags to Spirit Lake tonight," he said to divert her, "but Bill said they'll be there tomorrow for sure. In the meantime," he added, pulling open a bureau drawer and taking out a pair of blue cotton pajamas, "I'll share these with you." He tossed the shirt to her.

Katherine instinctively reached out and caught it. She held it out in front of her and eyed it dubiously. "We'll share?"

"Sure—you'll wear the tops and I'll wear the bottoms." Josh shrugged out of his shirt, rolled it into a ball, and tossed it into the wicker basket in the corner that served as a hamper. "They're brand-new—my grandmother gave them to me for Christmas one year and I've never worn them. I don't usually wear pajamas," he added, laughter crinkling the corners of his eyes.

Katherine couldn't help it. Curiosity overrode her good sense. "Just what do you usually wear?"

"Nothing."

"Oh." An instant picture of Josh wearing absolutely nothing leapt to mind, and her entire body reacted with a surge of heat. She felt the warmth move up her throat and cheeks and knew that she was blushing. *I never blush! Why do I let him get to me like this?* Furious with herself, she forced her gaze to hold his. "I'll change in the bathroom."

"All right." Josh knew his blunt comment had embarrassed her, but he hadn't missed the instant awareness that had leapt into her eyes. As he watched her march out the door on her way to the bathroom across the hall, he felt a small twinge of remorse that he'd made her uncomfortable, but it subsided beneath the delight of discovering that he wasn't the only one struggling against attraction.

Whistling silently, he propped the pillows against the headboard and stretched out on the bed with a book to wait for her. When the door finally opened, he looked up from his page to find her entering the room wrapped in his blue robe once again. The collar and lapels of his pajama shirt peeked out from between the edges of the robe. Disappointed that the thick terry cloth swallowed her slim curves, he swung his legs over the edge of the bed and stood.

"I forgot to tell you that Mom left a brush and comb in here for you." He picked up the brush from the bureau top and handed it to her, smiling as she smoothed a hand self-consciously over her tousled hair.

"Thank you. Do you need help with your bandage?" she said as he walked past her and opened the door.

"No," he glanced at the square of white gauze in its sterile package lying on top of the blue pajama bottoms he held in one hand. "I'm getting liberated tonight. No more mummy wrappings—I've graduated to bandage squares."

Katherine frowned at the size of the sterile pad. "Are you sure?" she said skeptically. "That doesn't look large enough."

Josh shrugged. "As long as it covers the stitches, who cares?" His gaze stroked over her still worried face. "Stop worrying," he ordered gently. "Make yourself comfortable—I'll be back."

The door closed on his broad back and Katherine stood staring unblinkingly at the wood panels for several minutes.

"Comfortable," she muttered to herself, glaring at the pillows nestled cozily side by side at the head of the bed. She yanked the brush through the tangles in her hair, wincing as the bristles tugged against her scalp until each strand lay smooth and silky. She glanced in the mirror over the bureau and grimaced at her scrubbed face and the oversize robe wrapped around her body before she tossed the brush down on the bureau and turned her back on the mirror. With quick, efficient movements, she stripped the lightweight white spread from the bed and removed the top blanket. She dropped the blanket and one of the pillows on the thick, braided wool rug and replaced the spread, smoothing it neatly across the foot of the bed. It took only a few moments to straighten the blanket and shrug out of the robe.

Josh pushed open the bedroom door and stepped inside, closing it silently. Katherine was standing with her back to him, stretching across a pillow and a blanket spread on the floor to toss his blue robe over the arm of the overstuffed chair in the corner. The movement drew up the hem of the pajama shirt, exposing long shapely legs, the smooth line of her thigh, and a scant inch of white cotton panties. His throat went dry and he swallowed convulsively, his gaze fastened on the plain white elastic that hugged the curve of her bottom.

Katherine turned away from the chair and froze, her breath catching at the look in Josh's eyes. He leaned against the door, his arms crossed over his chest, the blue cotton pajama bottoms riding low on his hips below the stark white of the square bandage. Dark gold hair circled his navel and arrowed downward to disappear beneath the elasticized waistline of the pajamas. Drops of water glistened in his hair, and the air in the room was suddenly too close, scented with soap, after-shave, and the indefinable scent of man.

Josh tore his eyes away from her legs and the blue cotton that had slid downward to conceal the chaste, white cotton panties. His gaze wandered over the loose, too-big shirt, pausing to notice the long sleeves folded up over the delicate bones of her wrists, the soft blue cotton draped over her breasts, and the lapels that created a neckline that plunged to a deep vee before the first button clipped the edges together. He struggled to pull himself together and lifted his eyes to hers. The stunned awareness he found there almost sent him lunging away from the door toward her, but the underlying wariness in her green eyes kept his shoulders against the wooden panels.

Platonic. No sex. He repeated the words in a desperate litany inside his brain. Even as he said them, he wondered how long he could hold onto his sanity.

Katherine tensed when he pushed away from the closed door, but he only stalked to the head of the bed and threw back the covers.

"Do you need the light on?" he asked over his shoulder, his blue eyes pinning her with a glance that reflected iron control and a smoldering, frustrated awareness.

"No." She shook her head and dropped to her knees on the floor. She rolled herself in the blanket and lay perfectly still, holding her breath as the lamp switch clicked and the room was enveloped in darkness. The bed creaked faintly as it took Josh's weight and the sheet rustled softly as he slid beneath it. The silence held; he didn't argue with her about her bed on the floor, and she released her breath in a long sigh. For one long, breathless moment when she'd turned earlier and found him watching her from the door, she'd thought he was going to act on the smoldering desire that lit his eyes with banked blue fire.

But then he'd abruptly ignored her, and she wasn't sure if she was happy about that or not.

She stared at the ceiling, barely visible in the dark room. *You're the one who insisted on a "just friends" relationship. Did you want him to do something?* She wasn't sure. She knew that she wanted him to kiss her. Ever since that brief brush of lips in the police station in Mexico, she'd wondered if the sparks she'd felt would burst into flames if he kissed her again. Part of her wanted the opportunity to explore all the possibilities hinted at by that brief touching of mouths. But how could she safely explore kisses when they were both barely dressed in shared pajamas and enclosed in the private coziness of this bedroom?

I know this is only pretend, but there's something about taking vows and signing a marriage certificate, she admitted, frowning at the silent ceiling. *I've never felt this way about a man before.* She shifted, tugging the light blanket higher, refusing to allow her mind to contemplate the "L" word. It was just not possible that she could be falling in love with Josh McFadden; what she felt was surely a result of the intimacy of their situation. *It's perfectly normal for me to be attracted to him,* she told herself. *After all, he's very attractive, handsome even, and he has a body any woman would drool over.* But she'd known lots of handsome, well-built men, that tiny little nagging voice in the back of her mind reminded her. Her life until now had been well-ordered, structured, and slightly dull, and she couldn't deny that Josh's aura of danger fascinated her. The contrast between the dangerous outlaw who had rescued her in Mexico and the easygoing, laid-back man he had become when with his family was particularly intriguing. He'd slipped easily into his role as the youngest McFadden brother, and Katherine couldn't help but wonder which was the real Joshua. Perhaps, she mused, the answer was that he was both, and if so, he was far more complex than any other men of her acquaintance.

Sometime after midnight, Katherine fell asleep. Josh waited until she stopped tossing and turning; then he waited until another fifteen minutes had passed in slow silence before he pushed back the sheet and left the bed. This time, there was no creaking of bedsprings to mark his movements, and the braided rug gave no hint of his footsteps.

He knelt beside her. The room was too dark for him to see her clearly, but he could tell that she lay on her back with her arms outflung, the blanket kicked away from her bare limbs and feet. His pajama shirt was twisted around her waist, leaving only the modest cotton panties covering her from beneath the shadowed indentation of her navel to her thighs. His blood heated just from his looking at her, and he ruthlessly repressed the urge to stroke his palm over the bare, silky skin of her abdomen. Instead, he slid his arms beneath her knees and shoulders and gathered her into his arms, standing with one smooth surge of power.

She didn't awaken, not when he lifted her and not when he lowered her to the sheets and slid in beside her. Instead, she turned on her side and curled close to him, murmuring contentedly as her cheek found the warm skin of his shoulder. Josh eased an arm under her and she snuggled closer, nuzzling her face against his neck before she sighed, her soft curves going boneless against him.

Josh tensed, struggling with the nearly overwhelming need to find her mouth with his and ease some of the sexual torment that strung his body. But he forced himself to concentrate on relaxing, until finally, he was able to wrap his other arm around her waist and hug her closer, drifting into sleep himself with a sigh of contentment.

Katherine came awake slowly. She stretched, yawning, her toes curling against the smooth cotton of the sheet.

Something was wrong. She frowned, trying to remember. Memory niggled at the edge of her consciousness, forcing her eyelids up. Sleepy as she was, her lashes only made it halfway and she lay perfectly still, trying to absorb what she could see of the room through her half-closed eyes.

Sunlight streamed through the window, throwing a lace-patterned square of gold warmth across the end of the bed and her bare legs. She stared at the sunlight that gilded her legs on the white sheet for a long moment before realization sprang to life and her lashes flew upward. The sheet! She was lying on the sheet, on top of the mattress, on a bed that definitely wasn't her pallet on the floor.

She twisted her head sideways on her pillow and breathed a sigh of relief to find she was alone. But the dent in the other pillow told her that Josh hadn't spent the night on the floor. Clearly, they had spent the night together, in the same bed.

Oh, no. Her eyes squeezed shut in mortification before they flew open again. *Please, please, don't let me have done something stupid while I was asleep!* She didn't even remember climbing into bed with him. Heaven only knew what he must be thinking!

She sat up, realized that her borrowed pajama top was twisted around her waist, and grimaced. *Great! He certainly got an eyeful!* She pushed herself upright and swung her legs over the edge of the bed. *Oh, well,* she decided philosophically, *at least I had my undies on—I never wear any with my own pajamas.*

She shoved her hair out of her eyes and slid off the bed, catching Josh's blue robe up from the corner chair and tugging it on.

I wonder where he is.

By the time she'd showered, dressed in the green skirt and blouse, and applied makeup, Josh still hadn't appeared. She walked slowly down the stairs, trailing a hand along the silky-smooth wood of the bannister with appreciation. The aroma of coffee drew her down the hall to the back of the house and into the kitchen, and when she stepped through the door, she found Josh's mother, Jeannie, washing tomatoes at the sink.

Jeannie had been expecting Katherine ever since she heard the telltale creak of the stair tread halfway up the flight to the second floor, and she glanced over her shoulder, a welcoming smile dimpling her cheek.

"Hello, there. I was beginning to wonder if I should wake you." She dried her hands on a dish towel and swung away from the sink. "Josh told me you need a pot of coffee as soon as you wake up. Is that true?" Her eyes twinkled at Katherine as she poured a mug of coffee from the pot atop the stove, waving her free hand toward a chair. "Sit down, sit down. I'll bring this over."

"I'm afraid so," Katherine admitted, sinking into a ladder-back chair at the old-fashioned butcher-block table in the center of the big room. "Thank you," she said gratefully when Jeannie put the mug in front of her. The aromatic steam drifted upward and she sniffed, half closing her eyes in pure enjoyment. "That smells wonderful."

Jeannie chuckled and returned to the sink. "You remind me of my husband, Gavin. He sleepwalks for the first half hour he's awake every morning, until the caffeine jump-starts his system. And Melanie! That girl doesn't even open her eyes until she pours a few cups of coffee down her throat."

Katherine smiled and sipped her coffee, content to insert a "yes" or "no" here and there as Jeannie chatted on about her family and their predilection for coffee. Katherine was leaning her chin on her fist, watching a huge, orange tiger-striped cat doze in the sunshine on the floor beneath an open window, when voices sounded outside.

Jeannie craned her head to see out the window.

"There's Josh now, and Cole's with him."

Katherine tensed, straightening in her chair and clasping both hands around the mug on the table's scrubbed surface. Cole and Melanie were the only two family members she hadn't met yet. Everyone else—Gavin, Jeannie, Sarah, Jesse, little Jennifer, Trace, and Lily—had gathered at the old Victorian house the evening before to welcome Josh home and meet Katherine.

Josh stepped through the kitchen door first, and Katherine's gaze flew to meet his. The uncertainty in her eyes told him that she wasn't angry with him for moving her into bed with him the night before. Relieved, he crossed the room, and with the casual affection of a husband and lover, he dropped his arm across her shoulders and bent to brush her mouth with his.

"Good morning, Katy," he drawled with a heart-stopping smile. "Sleep well?"

"Yes, very," she managed to stammer out, her heart racing. Evidently he'd decided to go beyond holding hands and loving gazes. *Isn't this what I wanted?* she thought dizzily. *To have him kiss me safely outside the bedroom?* Except she didn't feel safe. Just the brief brush of his lips against hers had the blood fizzing through her veins and left her aching for more.

Josh watched the dazed expression on her face and wished suddenly, fiercely, that they were alone somewhere, anywhere, so he could kiss her again and find out if her mouth was really as sweet as that one swift taste. He forced himself to look away from her and found Cole's amused eyes taking in the fire that arced between him and his wife.

"I think I can safely assume that this is Katherine?" Cole said, and stepped past Josh to take her hand in his.

"Kate, this is my brother Cole," Josh said, his glance stroking over her flushed cheeks.

"Good morning, Cole. It's a pleasure to meet you," she said with quick composure, taking in Josh's oldest brother with one swift, assessing look. He was slightly taller than Josh, and he was more heavily muscled. He had the same wheat-blond hair as Sarah and Trace, paler than Josh's golden brown, but like all of the McFadden siblings, he had the unmistakable, thick-lashed, sapphire blue eyes that marked them as members of the clan. Like Josh, too, he had a clear, sharp integrity in the blue depths of his eyes. Katherine decided she liked Josh's brother and relaxed, smiling up at him.

Cole had been doing his own assessing, and he, too, liked what he saw. He still wasn't sure exactly what it was about Josh's attitude toward his new bride that struck him as slightly off-kilter, but after watching the sparks that they struck from each other, he decided that whatever it was, Josh would work it out.

"Well, Katherine, you can't be nearly as glad to meet me as I am to meet you," he said with a grin that was amazingly like Josh's. "I was beginning to think Josh was never going to stay in one place long enough to get married. Just exactly how did you manage it, anyway?"

Katherine slanted Josh a sideways look through her lashes before smiling back at Cole. "I made him an offer he couldn't refuse."

Josh choked on the coffee he was sipping from her mug. Katherine stood quickly and pummeled his back with her palm.

"What's the matter, sweetheart?" she asked innocently, standing so close to him that her breasts pressed against his forearm. "Did it go down the wrong way? Are you all right?"

Josh eyed her, wondering whether he ought to retaliate. But she was so damned cute, with her green eyes laughing at him while she looked at him with concern on her features, that he decided to let it ride. Besides, he'd be tempted to let her get away with anything as long as she was touching him. He set the mug back on the table, and before she could step away from him, he wrapped his arms around her and hugged her close.

"I'm fine, Katy." He kissed her cheek, his lips just touching the corner of her mouth, relishing the shiver that went through the warm curves pressed against him, before lifting his head to wink at Cole. "Actually, Cole, we made each other offers that neither of us could refuse."

"Oh, yeah?" Cole hadn't missed the exchanged glances and had the feeling that there was more to the story than either was admitting. 'Well, it's easy to see why you wanted Katherine, but what could you possibly have to offer her that she couldn't refuse?"

Katherine felt Josh's arms tighten as if to ward off a blow and she tilted her head back to smile up at him before she answered Cole.

"Why, himself, of course," she said softly, and the taut body she lay against relaxed.

"I'm not sure you got such a great bargain," Cole teased, laughing as Josh's eyes narrowed threateningly.

"I'm going to have to talk to Melanie," Josh said mildly, enjoying the feel of Katherine resting trustingly in his arms. "She doesn't know what she's getting into by marrying you."

"Yes, she does," Cole said complacently, a look of warm contentment flitting across his features, "and just like Katherine and you, she's marrying me anyway."

"If you two don't stop sniping at each other, Katherine's going to think she's married into a horrible family,'' Jeannie said, just as the sound of slamming car doors and the murmur of feminine voices drifted through the open windows. Once again, she peered out the window above the sink. "Sarah's here with Jennifer—and Melanie, too.''

Cole reached the door just as Sarah walked through it, little Jennifer tucked against her shoulder. The tiny baby was wearing a pink sunsuit with ruffles across her diapered bottom, and her big blue eyes stared unblinkingly at the adults.

"Hi, Mom, Josh. Hello, Katherine, I'm glad to see you survived the gathering of the clan last night!" Sarah breezed into the room with her usual cheerfulness.

Jeannie immediately took Jennifer from her and began to coo at the baby, laughing as the little girl blew happy bubbles in reply.

From the shelter of Josh's encircling arms, Katherine watched Cole greet a lovely, green-eyed brunette and saw the melting tenderness on his face as he brushed her mouth with his. That she returned his affection was obvious.

Cole drew the woman further into the kitchen to introduce her, and Josh reluctantly released Katherine when she unobtrusively wriggled to be free. He watched as she chatted with Melanie and then Sarah, and his heart caught in his throat when she took Jennifer from Jeannie and cradled her. Katherine's features softened as she held the tiny girl, one palm cupping the silky head as she whispered to her.

That should be our baby. The thought leapt unbidden into Josh's mind and he squeezed his eyes shut in rejection. *We're not really married. She's not my wife. We won't have babies together,* he reminded himself, and lifted his lashes to find Katherine staring at him, her irises gone deep green with an unconscious longing that pulled at him. Suddenly, he wanted her out of there. As much as he loved his family, and missed them when he was away, it wasn't his mother, father, sister, or brothers he needed. It was Katherine. *I get to have her for only nine days*, he realized suddenly, *and three of those days are already gone*.

With an abruptness that startled the rest of the group, he crossed the room and plucked Jennifer from Katherine and deposited her in Sarah's arms.

"Sorry, Mom," he said, catching Katherine's hand and threading his fingers through hers, suffering a shock at the unexpected intimacy of the contact. "I promised Katy that I'd show her CastleRock today. We're having lunch out and then we're going to pick up our luggage." He tugged Katherine out the kitchen door and she called good-bye over her shoulder.

The four adults left standing in the kitchen were speechless for a moment before they exchanged glances and grinned.

"I think maybe Josh wanted Katherine to himself for a while," Sarah said, patting Jennifer's back with a soothing hand.

"I think maybe you're right," Cole drawled with a very male grin. "I can certainly relate to that." He leered at Melanie.

"Stop that!" She laughed, a pink flush moving up her throat.

Jeannie eyed them with resignation. "Does that mean you two are skipping lunch, too?"

Cole opened his mouth to say yes, but Melanie clapped her slim fingers over his lips to stop him.

"No, it does not," she said, smiling up at him as he took advantage of the opportunity to nibble on her fingers. "I have only an hour until I have to be back at the shop."

"Damn." Cole sighed and pressed a kiss into her palm. "I can't wait until we're married."

"Me, too," she said softly.

"Well, in that case," Jeannie said briskly, turning toward the refrigerator, "you can set the table, Cole, and, Melanie, you can get the sun tea from the back porch. It should be ready to drink by now."

Katherine let Josh tug her after him down the sidewalk that led around the side of the house and across the lawn to the garage. She had to take running steps to keep up with his long strides, and when they entered the dim garage and he released her, it took a few moments for her eyes to become adjusted to the lack of brilliant sunlight. When they did, she found Josh holding open the door of a gleaming black Porsche.

Astonished, she stared, first at the car and then at Josh.

"What's the matter?" he asked.

"Well, it's just not what I expected." She waved a hand in confusion at the sleek car. "Not after the jeep and the motorcycle. I just . . ." She glanced from the car to Josh's impassive face.

"It's not mine," he said. "It's Cole's. He's letting me drive it while I'm home—I didn't think you'd want to ride the bike all the time."

"Oh." She nodded, wondering what he was thinking as he stood watching her without expression. "That was nice of him," she added uncertainly.

"Yeah," Josh replied, holding the door open while she slid onto the leather-covered bucket seat, before bending to tuck in her skirt.

His bent head was at eye level for Katherine. His gaze flicked up and he froze, their gazes snared as they stared into each other's eyes. Hearts beat faster, breath shortened, mouths went dry as they fought the desire that flared between them.

Josh was the first to recover. He forced his gaze away from the deep pools of her eyes, and with one last, hot glance at the soft curve of her mouth, he stepped back and closed the door with tightly leashed control. If he didn't kiss her soon, he was going to explode, he thought grimly.

Katherine didn't speak as he reversed the powerful car out of the garage and down the driveway to the street. Covertly, she watched the play of thigh muscles beneath the faded denim of his jeans as he depressed the clutch, and the subtle flexing of his biceps as he shifted the sophisticated, high-powered car with the same expert ease she'd noticed when she'd ridden with him across the desert in the battered jeep and down the narrow Minnesota and Iowa highways on the motorcycle.

The hand closed over the gearshift knob was long-fingered and strong, with clean, pared nails and a dusting of golden-brown hair on the wrist and forearm. She didn't remember noticing men's hands and arms before, but something about Josh's made her stomach tighten, and started a strange awareness trembling through her midriff.

He drove without speaking, and Katherine stared

out her lowered window at the broad, residential streets flying by. They left the well-kept little town behind and took a tree-shaded road that wound around the lakeshore. Katherine glanced sideways at him, wanting to ask him where they were going, but the tight set of his mouth discouraged her and she turned silently back to the view.

Josh downshifted, slowing the sports car to a crawl before he turned off the highway onto a bumpy graveled lane that twisted and wound through a tangle of trees and brush until it widened to reveal a sandy beach and the sunlit, ruffled expanse of lake that stretched beyond.

Confused, Katherine glanced around at the deserted shoreline and then back at Josh.

"Where are we?"

"Lookout Point," he said, and twisted the ignition key. The engine noise died away, leaving only the soft lap of the waves against the shore and the sigh of the gentle breeze through the trees to pierce the silence.

Katherine's heart thudded against her ribs. "What are we doing here?"

Josh's gaze left the windshield and fastened on her face. "When I was a kid, we called this place Makeout Point."

"Oh." Katherine felt her whole body heat.

"I brought you here because we have to talk, and we can't do that at my folks' place with people walking in and out every other minute."

"Oh." Disappointment flooded her, dulling the breathless anticipation that had buoyed her only moments before.

Josh's eyes narrowed and his control slipped another notch.

"But first, I'm going to kiss you." He watched her eyes widen, the irises going dark emerald green. "If you don't want it, now's the time to tell me."

SIX

She didn't answer. She didn't need to. Josh watched her lips part, saw the quickened rush of her pulsebeat at her throat, registered the slight yearning lean of her body toward his, and felt the last vestiges of his iron control dissolve.

"Katherine." Her name was a half groan, half growl from his lips as he reached for her.

Katherine didn't protest when his hands closed over her shoulders and propelled her forward to meet his descending mouth. She didn't hear the throaty sigh of pure pleasure and relief that purred deep in her throat as his lips found hers. She only knew that at last her curiosity was being satisfied and it was everything she'd hoped for. His lips were warm, his mouth moving against hers with an urgent demand she couldn't deny, and she sank against him, her hands lifting to trace the heated skin of his face before her fingers moved into the thick softness of his hair.

Josh buried his mouth against hers, lost in the taste and scent and feel of her. But it wasn't enough, and he wrapped his arms around her, hauling her across the car's console and onto his lap. The round curve of her bottom fit into his lap, her breasts cushioned against his chest, and he anchored one hand in her hair, his fingers threading through the silky mane to cradle her head. His other hand closed over her hipbone and he crushed her against him, desperate to have her as close as humanly possible.

At last, he had to lift his mouth from hers to let them both breathe. Her golden-brown lashes fluttered and slowly lifted, the dazed wonder that lay in her green eyes slamming into his heart like a sledgehammer.

"Katherine," he murmured huskily. "We have to talk."

A slow, sultry smile lifted the corners of her mouth. "Yes," she replied, her breath ghosting over lips that were still damp from his, "we do." Her lashes flickered down, her gaze lingering on his mouth before it lifted to meet his again. "But do you think you could kiss me again first?"

His heart stopped, then accelerated, shuddering against his ribs with a beat that drummed in his ears. "If I kiss you first, I'm afraid we won't ever get around to talking."

She eyed him gravely, her fingers unconsciously making little caressing movements against his nape. "I'm afraid if we talk first, you won't kiss me anymore."

"Would that bother you?" His voice rasped over a throat gone dry with need.

DETACH AND MAIL CARD TODAY–

FIRST CLASS MAIL

OFFICIAL ENTRY CARD

Kismet Romances
"$1,000,000+ Sweepstakes"
PO Box 7249
PHILA PA 19101-9895

PLACE
POSTAGE
STAMP
HERE

"Yes." She nodded slowly, her gaze fastened on his. "It would."

"Good," he murmured, "because it sure as hell would bother me." He gave in to the lure of her lips so near and brushed her mouth with his. Reluctantly, he forced himself to keep it brief. They still needed to talk. "We have to talk about this, honey."

"About what?" Katherine asked hazily, her senses still spinning.

"About kissing, and sharing a bed."

"Oh." Her eyes rounded with comprehension, but she didn't stiffen and move away from him.

"I'll be honest with you, sweetheart. I've had a hell of a time keeping my hands off you ever since Mexico, but I promised you I wouldn't do anything you didn't want, and you said you wanted a strictly platonic relationship." Beneath half-lowered lids, his blue eyes gleamed nearly black with arousal. "I know I told you I wanted you to bat your eyelashes at me and pretend to be crazy about me, but I get the definite impression that it's not all acting. Am I wrong?"

Katherine stared up at him. He was asking her to bare her emotions and be completely honest with him. Never before had she let a man that close, but he was offering to do the same and she could do no less. "No," she said, her voice husky with emotion. "You're not wrong."

He sucked in a deep breath and held it while he fought to keep from kissing her in sheer relief. Only the knowledge that once he started kissing her again he doubted that he could stop long enough to finish this conversation, kept him from doing just that.

"Good," he managed to get out. "So we're

agreed this feeling is mutual. I think we better decide what we're going to do about it.''

''Do about it? I don't understand. Aren't we doing something about it now?'' she asked, confused.

''Yeah, but what about tonight?''

''What about tonight?''

''What about when we go to bed tonight? I can guarantee you that if we start kissing in bed, I'm not going to want to stop with just kisses.''

''Oh.'' Katherine hadn't thought beyond the sheer pleasure of kissing and holding him since he parked the car, but reality returned with a vengeance and her eyes widened and lost their drowsiness. She stiffened and would have pulled away from him, but his arms tightened and refused to let her go.

''Don't,'' he said, his voice half command, half plea. ''I know I got us into this situation and that it's all my fault that we're caught in this sham marriage, but now that we're here, it's going to take both of us cooperating to make it through.''

''What do you mean?'' she asked, watching him through her lashes.

''I mean we've got two choices. You can leave, right now, and I won't stop you.''

Katherine's heart dropped like a stone at his words.

''Do you want me to leave?''

Josh stared at her for a long moment before he answered. ''No,'' he said, the words husky with desire, his fingers moving in unconscious, compulsive circles against her waist. ''No, I don't want you to leave.''

''What's our other choice?'' she asked, her heart settling with relief.

"The other choice is, you stay, and we try to find a way to survive the remaining days without making love."

Katherine stared at him, a tiny frown growing, her lips slowly drooping with disappointment. "Why?"

"Why?" It was Josh's turn to look confused. "Because if you don't leave, the only other option is, you stay."

"No," she said with a little shrug of exasperation. "Why can't we make love?"

Josh swore under his breath, his whole body clenching at her words. "Damn it," he ground out, "don't say things like that. I'm trying to be a gentleman here, and you know why we can't make love."

"No, I don't," she insisted softly, stubbornly.

He heaved a sigh and glared at her. "Because in six more days, you go back to Mexico and get a divorce, remember? Unless you're telling me that you want a six-day affair. Do you?"

Katherine had temporarily forgotten all about the divorce part of their agreement. Her body hummed with desire, her nerve ends tingling with impatience for their conversation to end so that they could get back to the kissing and hugging. But Josh's words reminded her of the planned brevity of their relationship, and it was a distinct shock.

"No," she said slowly, consideringly, "no, I don't want an affair." She was beginning to suspect that she didn't want a Mexican divorce, either, but clearly, Josh wasn't contemplating anything more permanent.

"Right." Josh had known she would feel that way, but disappointment still settled in a heavy lump in the pit of his stomach. "So we need to set limits."

"We do?" She eyed him wistfully before conceding. "All right, if you say so."

"You aren't making this easy," he murmured, closing his eyes with sheer pleasure as her fingers moved in little caresses against his nape.

"No?" she whispered.

"No." He forced his lashes up and looked down into eyes that were warm, dark green pools of unconcealed desire.

"I'm sorry," she said softly, watching his lips move as he spoke. "What were you saying?"

He struggled to remember. "Limits," he managed to get out.

"Oh, yes. Limits." She ran the tip of her tongue over her lips in unconscious provocation. "I suppose kissing is out?" she asked wistfully.

"Uhmm, out," he murmured, distracted, even as invisible strings of desire shimmered between them and tugged his head lower until his breath mingled with the quick, uneven rush of hers across her parted lips. "Definitely—out." His lips lightly touched hers, the tip of his tongue delicately tracing the path hers had taken seconds before.

"Josh," Katherine breathed, her eyes drifting closed with pleasure as his lips explored hers before moving to brush tasting, butterfly kisses at the corners of her mouth and across her cheek, the bridge of her nose, and her closed eyelids.

"What, honey?" he whispered against the soft skin just below her ear.

"Are you sure kissing has to be off limits?" she asked, tilting her head to give him better access to the sensitive skin he was exploring.

"No," he ground out, burying his face in the

scented thickness of her hair. "Hell, no. You want kissing, you got it. I'll take anything you're willing to give me."

And he lifted his head, allowing her a brief glimpse of blue eyes that were nearly black with desire, his face flushed with heat. Then he took her mouth with his, and Katherine stopped thinking. She was incapable of thinking, she could only feel.

Long, satisfying moments later, Josh lifted his head and looked down at her. Her head lay against his shoulder, the soft fullness of her mouth bare of lipstick and faintly swollen from the pressure of his. Her cheeks were flushed with color, her eyes drowsy with pleasure, and he smiled, a slow, tender lift of his lips that reflected the possessiveness in his eyes.

"Maybe we should start this conversation all over again," he said, his fingers gentle as he brushed a silky swath of hair from her cheek. "I know you don't want an affair. And I know you *do* want kisses. But that still leaves a lot of unexplored territory in between."

In between. Katherine gazed up at him without speaking. Could she safely explore the way he made her feel? Was it possible that they could share kisses without losing control and burning each other to ashes in the fire? If they went their separate ways after Cole's wedding, she didn't want to carry with her a broken heart. On the other hand, if she passed up this opportunity to find out if the way he made her feel was real and lasting, would she ever get another chance?

"Katherine?" His husky voice held a question.

"Unexplored territory," she said thoughtfully, still faintly breathless. "I suppose there are a lot of—

possibilities—between holding hands and making love.''

His lips quirked in a wry grin. "Yeah, I would agree with that.''

"Do I have to give you specifics?'' She wasn't sure herself just how far she wanted to take this.

"Well,'' he drawled, reading her reticence in the sweep of lowered lashes and heightened color, "maybe not specifics, but I think we have to set some parameters so we both understand where the limits are.''

"All right.'' She nodded. "That seems sensible.''

Josh smothered a grin. *You'd think we were negotiating a grocery list!* "I assume that making love is out of bounds?''

Katherine nodded.

"Damn,'' he said with resignation. "Well, maybe we can play the rest by ear—how would that be?''

She lifted her gaze from the pulse that throbbed at the base of his throat and met his eyes. "That, uhm, that sounds fine.''

Josh watched her lashes drift lower and felt the stroke of her gaze running with obvious fascination over his lips. *This is not a good idea*, he tried to lecture himself. *Just kissing her could easily become addictive, and I'll have to let her go in only six days.* Still, he couldn't resist the lure of her willing mouth so close beneath his, and with a silent groan of despair, he lowered his head and kissed her again.

Not making love to her was turning out to be the most exquisite kind of torture, Josh thought grimly, watching Katherine. Seated across the room on the sofa by his mother, she turned the pages of the family photograph album and listened to Jeannie explain each picture.

"And this is Joshua at his fifth birthday party," Jeannie said, a fond smile of remembrance softening her features. "Wasn't he a handsome little boy?"

"Yes," Katherine agreed wholeheartedly, "he certainly was." She glanced up from the photo to find Josh staring at her intently. The handsome little boy grinning mischievously at the camera had grown into an even more handsome man, with a smile that was lethal, she reflected.

His lashes lowered, his glance drifting to her mouth before flicking back to her eyes, and Katherine flushed. The message in his darkened blue gaze was so obvious that she instinctively looked at his mother to see if she had noticed. But Jeannie was sifting through a stack of loose photographs tucked between the pages of the album and wasn't looking at either of them.

The clatter of boots sounded on the stairs, and Cole paused in the doorway to the living room.

"Melanie and I are meeting Sarah and Jesse and Trace and Lily at Big Eddie's Truck Stop. Josh, why don't you and Katherine come, too?"

Jeannie glared at her eldest son. "Eddie Lawson serves nothing but heart-attack food at that Truck Stop! Why, I bet there's not one healthy thing in the place except for the tomato and lettuce he puts on those greasy hamburgers!"

Cole and Josh exchanged grins.

"Mom," Cole said soothingly, "we're not going to eat there. We're going to have a couple of beers and dance to the jukebox in the bar next door."

"Hmmph," Jeannie sniffed, unconvinced. "If you

want to dance, why don't you go out to the Lake-Shore? It's much nicer.''

"Because Big Eddie's has cold beer and hot music, Mom." Cole winked at Katherine. "And both Melanie and Sarah have fond memories of the place."

Jeannie sniffed in disbelief.

Josh looked at Katherine. If he remembered correctly, the jukebox at Big Eddie's also had some slow, sultry tunes that were great to slow-dance to, and anything that gave him an excuse to hold Katherine close sounded good.

"Katherine?" he said, catching her glance. "Do you want to join them?"

"I'd love to." She smiled meltingly at him. Dancing sounded good, she thought to herself; maybe there would be some slow songs and he'd hold her close. Maybe they'd explore some of those as-yet-untried possibilities that lay between kissing and making love. A dance floor was safe—they couldn't get too carried away in a public place.

"Great." Josh surged out of his seat and caught Katherine's hand to tug her off the sofa. "We'll see you later, Mom, Dad."

"Good night, Jeannie—Gavin," Katherine called over her shoulder as he hustled her through the doorway to the hall.

The front screen door slapped shut and silence descended on the house. Jeannie closed the photo album and glanced up to see Gavin looking over the tops of his reading glasses at her, his blue eyes twinkling with amusement.

"What?" she demanded.

"I was just thinking," he said, laughter underlying

his deep tones. He carefully refolded the newspaper and laid it on the floor beside the recliner, took off his glasses and slid them onto the gleaming wood of the reading table, and pushed himself out of the chair to stalk toward her. "This is the first time in days that you and I have had the house to ourselves." He planted a hand against the sofa cushion on each side of her thighs. "I was beginning to think I was going to have to bribe them with a quarter and send them all to the movies to get you to myself."

Jeannie laughed and slid sideways on the sofa, tugging him down on top of her. "I'm not sure a quarter would work—inflation, you know." She stopped laughing and a frown creased her brow. "Gavin, do you notice anything a little—well, *odd* about Josh and Katherine?"

Gavin stopped nibbling on her earlobe and lifted his head to look down at her. "Odd? What do you mean, odd?"

"I don't know." She shrugged, unable to verbalize exactly what she meant. "I just get the feeling that there's something not quite right with them."

"The only thing I notice," Gavin said with a purely male grin of understanding, "is that he looks at her like a starving man with a full-course meal just out of reach. And she looks at him like she's about to melt into a puddle at his feet. That's not odd, honey, that's perfectly normal. They've only been married a few days and they ought to be off on a desert island for a few months with no distractions."

"I've noticed that, but are you sure that's all?" Jeannie asked, not entirely convinced.

"I'm sure. Stop worrying, honey. He's married,

isn't he? And I like Katherine. I think she's going to be good for him.''

"Are you sure?''

"I'm sure.'' Gavin smoothed a hand over Jeannie's little frown wrinkles and gently erased them. He was rewarded with a smile and bent to kiss her.

"Will you and Josh be living at his apartment in Houston, Katherine?'' Sarah asked, leaning her elbows on the round wooden table and fixing her new sister-in-law with an inquisitive stare.

"I'm not sure. We haven't really decided yet,'' Katherine said. *I didn't even know he had an apartment in Houston!* She tucked a strand of blond hair behind her ear, fiddled with the heart locket that hung on its silver chain around her neck, and straightened the off-the-shoulder sleeves of her white knit top before she realized that she was fidgeting nervously. With an effort, she forced herself to calmly fold her hands together on top of the table.

"Are you from Houston, Katherine?'' Melanie asked with curiosity. "Is that where you met Josh?''

"No, I'm from Boston, actually, and we met in a little town in Mexico. Josh more or less saved my life.''

"Really?'' Lily's lavender eyes lit with interest. "That sounds intriguing—tell us how.''

"I was in a small town in the interior and the friend I was with drank too much and drove off and left me—with no money and no transportation back to Santa Rosa. Josh was kind enough to get me out of what could have been a very sticky situation.''

"I always knew Josh was a hero—not that he ever tells us anything about his escapades,'' Sarah said wryly. "But now you can keep track of him for us. Were you vacationing in Mexico?"

Katherine nodded, her fingers pleating her napkin into little folds. She glanced quickly toward the bar, where the four men stood waiting for their order to be filled. She gave a quick prayer that Josh had stuck as close as possible to the truth when he answered questions from his family, and hoped their stories meshed. "In a manner of speaking. I was visiting my father, who's filming in Santa Rosa."

"Filming?" Sarah broke in with interest. "Is your father in the movie industry?"

"Yes," Katherine said warmly. Her family was a safe subject and she gave a silent sigh of relief. "My father is Charles Logan, and he's a producer."

"Of course," Lily said with surprise. "I love his work."

"My goodness." Melanie smiled at Katherine. "I'm almost afraid to ask you what your mother does."

Katherine smiled fondly. "My mother is Katherine Bennington-Logan, and she spends most of her time administering the Bennington family trust in Boston."

"Katherine Bennington of Boston." Lily's eyes narrowed in thought. "I think I may have met her at a benefit concert some years ago—no, on second thought, I think the woman I'm remembering was named Adelaide, Adelaide Bennington."

"Adelaide is my great-aunt." Katherine laughed, her eyes twinkling at Lily. "And if you met her, it's no wonder you remember the name. She's quite a grand old lady."

"The woman I remember was outspoken and a

trifle eccentric''—Lily grinned at Katherine—''and completely unforgettable.''

''That's my great-aunt.'' Katherine chuckled. ''Very few people forget Adelaide.''

''Who's Adelaide?'' Josh's deep voice interrupted.

Katherine looked up to find him standing at her shoulder, a frosty mug of beer in each hand. He was wearing snug jeans and loafers, and a short-sleeved blue knit polo shirt that made his deep tan appear even darker. Jesse, Cole, and Trace were right behind him.

''My great-aunt. You remember, Josh, I told you about her.'' Her eyes flashed him a warning and he grinned down at her.

''Of course,'' he said smoothly. ''Great-Aunt Adelaide.'' He slid the two mugs he carried onto the tabletop in front of her and dropped down into the vacant captain's chair beside her.

''I met her at a concert in Boston,'' Lily told him, smiling her thanks at Trace when he handed her a mug of beer.

''No kidding.'' Josh draped an arm over the back of Katherine's chair and leaned closer. ''What a small world.''

The other three couples at the table saw Katherine blush and the heated sideways glance she gave Josh and exchanged knowing, indulgent smiles.

''I think we should dance,'' Cole announced, taking pity on Josh, and pushed back his chair and stood. ''C'mon, woman.''

''Yes, Your Highness,'' Melanie said with a laugh, and obeyed his hand that caught hers and urged her up beside him.

Josh watched the table rapidly empty before he

leaned over Katherine, his lips brushing her ear as he whispered, "Wanna dance?"

Katherine turned her head and their faces were nearly touching at lips, noses, and foreheads. "Do you?" she breathed, her eyes smiling into his.

"I can think of other things I'd rather be doing," he said, glancing with meaning at her mouth, "but since we can't, I'll settle for dancing."

Katherine's temperature shot skyward. "All right," she managed to say breathlessly.

Josh's arm left the back of her chair and he stood, catching her hand and threading her fingers through his to tug her after him onto the dance floor. He didn't release her fingers when he paused and turned her into his arms; instead, he tugged her arm around his neck and only released her to wrap both of his arms around her waist.

Katherine linked her hands at his nape and didn't protest when he pulled her close until their bodies fit snugly from head to thigh, their legs brushing as they swayed to the slow, dreamy music.

The dance floor was small, tucked into a far corner of the bar, and the low-ceilinged room was dimly lit and sparsely populated. It occurred to Josh that in all likelihood, Big Eddie's Truck Stop was probably nothing like the type of upscale cocktail lounge that Katherine was used to.

He tipped his head back to look down into her face. "Do you mind being here—in the bar, I mean?"

Confusion flickered across Katherine's features. "Why should I mind?"

"It just occurred to me that it's probably less . . .

sophisticated than the kind of bar you're used to in Boston.''

Katherine glanced around the room, noting the few truckers in boots and jeans quietly nursing their beers at the bar, and the two middle-aged couples who chatted and shared a booth across the room.

''You mean because there aren't any hanging green ferns and brass and glass tables?'' she asked, slanting a teasing glance at him from beneath the shield of her thick lashes.

''Does that mean you don't mind?'' Josh answered her question with a question.

''Yes,'' she said, her voice husky from the tantalizing press of his hard body against hers and the rhythmic brush of his long legs against hers, bare beneath the hem of her short linen skirt. ''I don't mind.'' A thought occurred to her and this time it was she who tipped her head back to look at him. ''Why did you ask me that? Do you think I'm a snob? That I only enjoy expensive, glitzy places?''

''No,'' he denied quickly, his voice carrying a quiet certainty that soothed her suspicions. ''I may have thought that when I first met you, but you've been a good sport about everything from the desert heat and sand to riding on the back of my bike, not to mention covering for me with this fake marriage.'' His mouth curved in an approving, affectionate smile and his eyes heated as one hand stroked up the curve of her back to slide into the thickness of her hair at her nape. ''No, honey, I wouldn't make the mistake of thinking you're a snob—it's just that I'm not Boston society, and you are. I don't think an ordinary workingman's bar is the type of place you usually frequent, is it?''

"No," Katherine whispered, struggling to cope with a fierce surge of emotion at his words of approval, "it's not, but that doesn't mean I couldn't grow accustomed to the practice."

Josh's heart clenched in reaction. How he wished he could believe that, but he knew the dream of an ordinary man like him marrying a princess just couldn't come true.

"No—variety is fun for a while, but as a lifestyle—" He broke off and left the sentence unfinished. "Didn't someone famous once say, 'I've been rich and I've been poor, and rich is better'?"

"I'm not rich," Katherine told him.

"Your family is," Josh reminded her.

"Not really. There's the trust, of course, and my father earns a good income, but we aren't really *rich*."

Josh wondered briefly just exactly how much money she thought someone had to have to qualify for *rich*.

Katherine eyed his expression and knew he was unconvinced. She wondered briefly just exactly how much money he thought she had. She opened her mouth to tell him that her own income was a yearly stipend from her grandmother's trust fund and a comfortable salary from her work as an administrator for the Bennington trust. But then she realized that she was willing to give it up if he would only consider making this sham marriage real. Her mouth closed without her saying a word, so startled was she at the direction her unguarded thoughts were taking.

"I'm really just a working girl," she said instead, but the disbelief on Josh's face told her that he wasn't convinced.

"If you say so, sweetheart." He tucked her closer and whispered against her temple. "Right now, I don't care how rich you are. All I want to think about is this minute, this second, and how good it feels to hold you."

His mouth brushed tasting little kisses against her temple and cheek. She smiled in pleasure and sighed as he dropped his head to nuzzle the bare slope of her shoulders.

"You like that?" he murmured, smiling against silky skin.

"Mmmhh." She closed her eyes, her fingers rubbing against his scalp with tactile pleasure. "Yes. Definitely."

"Me, too." Reluctantly, he lifted his head. "Too much."

The slow, dreamy strains of the country ballad they danced to trailed off into silence, but Josh didn't release her and they stood in each other's arms, waiting for the music to start again. When it did, the fast, hard-driving beat startled them both.

"Hey, Josh," Trace called as he swung Lily in a quick Texas two-step. "You can't slow-dance to this music!"

"Who the hell picked this?" Josh growled before he shot an exasperated look at his oldest brother. "Let me guess—it had to be Cole."

"What? You don't like Hank Williams, Jr.?" Cole grinned. "This is great stuff, little brother."

"Since when did you like country-swing dancing?" Josh asked, watching as Cole twirled Melanie, her green eyes glowing, her cheeks flushed with the exertion.

"Since Melanie decided it looked like fun and

made me take lessons. Too bad you don't know how, Josh.''

Josh's eyes narrowed over Cole before he looked down at Katherine. "Do you know how to dance like that?" he asked her quietly.

Katherine's glance left the other couples and lifted to meet his. "Actually, yes."

"You do?" It was the last thing Josh had expected. Waltzing, sure, the fox-trot, certainly, but country dancing?

Katherine chuckled at the look of surprise on his handsome features. "Just because I'm from Boston doesn't mean I only learned the waltz." She knew from the quick, embarrassed look he gave her that he had thought exactly that. "I met all kinds of people when I visited my father on location. Some were professional dancers and choreographers, and some of them just liked to dance." She leaned closer and said throatily, "You'd be surprised at all the things I know, Mr. McFadden."

Josh swallowed convulsively and fought the urge to throw her over his shoulder and haul her off to the nearest bed to find out exactly what she knew.

"Hmm." He cleared his throat and managed to breathe. "Can I assume that you know how to line-dance?"

"Yup." She grinned at him and stepped back. She waited a moment for the music and moved to her right in a quick grapevine. He rewarded her with a wide, mischievous grin and tugged her back beside him.

"Hey, Cole," he called.

"What?"

"Dance classes are all right, but if you really want

to learn country-swing, you need to learn it in a Texas honky-tonk.''

"Oh, yeah?" Cole laughed.

"Yeah. That's where Katy and I learned, didn't we, honey?''

"Yup," Katherine parroted, and when he kicked one booted foot out and stepped sideways, she followed him with perfect imitation, smiling up into his laughing eyes.

"I want to do that!" Lily demanded, and tugged Trace with her so they could line up beside Katherine and Josh.

"Me, too," chimed in Sarah and Melanie, and they pulled Jesse and Cole with them.

"The trick is to stay in line and don't trip up,'' Josh instructed as he and Katherine moved smoothly to the left. The other three couples followed, copying their steps.

By the time the song had ended, all of them were slightly breathless, laughing as someone missed a step and tripped, jostling the line of bobbing, kicking, sidestepping dancers.

"Let's do it again," Melanie demanded, shoving her hair out of her eyes and fanning her flushed face with a slender hand.

"Sounds good to me." Cole dug into his pocket for change and punched the buttons on the jukebox.

The smooth, solid beat of K. T. Oslin's "Come Next Monday" poured out of the speakers, and as the group quickly re-formed into a line, one of the truckers slid off his stool.

"Hell," he drawled, "I can't let y'all have all the fun—let me show you how we do it in Austin.''

Before the last guitar licks faded away, three more

truckers had joined them and the two middle-aged couples had deserted their booth to form a second line behind the first. The guffaws and giggles as the four struggled to follow Josh and Katherine's lead were interspersed with shouts of laughter as their feet tangled and they ran into one another.

"I didn't know this was supposed to be a contact sport," Cole said to Josh as the song ended and he stepped right and ran into Melanie as she stepped left.

"It's not." Josh grinned and slid an arm around Katherine's waist to pull her against him. "But the way you do it, it's beginning to look like one."

Cole aimed a good-natured punch at Josh's shoulder and he dodged it easily.

"These McFaddens." Melanie's green gaze met Katherine's with indulgent patience. "With them, everything is a contest. You should see them play football!" She rolled her eyes skyward.

"Touch football," Cole corrected her, and kissed the tip of her nose. "That's what we should do on Sunday, Josh—get together a game of touch."

"Don't volunteer," Melanie warned Katherine emphatically. "They claim they don't tackle—but they do! You'll wind up minus skin!"

"Nah, we'll look out for her," Josh said, eyeing Katherine. He wouldn't mind tackling her, he thought longingly, but not on the middle of a field with two opposing teams surrounding them.

The music started again, interrupting them, and the four were tugged back into line.

Hours later, Josh pulled the Porsche into the garage and switched off the engine. The sudden silence was broken only by the slight tick and soft rasp of the car settling. Katherine was snuggled into the bucket seat, her eyes closed, her hair spilling in a silvery fall across the black leather of the seatback.

"We're home, Katy," he said softly and was rewarded by the slight upward curve of her lips in a sleepy smile.

"Are we?" she said drowsily, refusing to open her eyes.

Josh leaned sideways and brushed his mouth against the curve of her smile. "Yeah," he murmured huskily, "we are."

"Oh."

His mouth continued to brush tiny, openmouthed kisses against her cheek and temple until he returned to her mouth. She smiled in pleasure and he kissed the upward tilt of her lips.

"You like that?" he murmured, his smile touching hers.

"Mmmhh." She sighed against his lips. "Yes. More, please."

His mouth teased hers until she slid her arms tightly around his neck and attempted to press him closer.

His mouth lifted a breath away from hers. "What's the matter?" he whispered huskily.

"You know what's wrong," she accused him throatily. "Don't tease."

She didn't have to ask twice. His arms tightened and his mouth dropped to take hers in a hot, wet kiss that went on and on until neither of them could breathe. At last, Josh tore his mouth from hers and buried his face against the curve of her shoulder.

"Damn," he ground out. "I want more than kisses."

Katherine's arms tightened, her body shaking with the same frustrated need that trembled through him.

"I do, too," she confessed, her voice a throaty breath of sound in his ear.

"What the hell are we going to do about this?" he groaned.

SEVEN

"I don't know," she confessed, tilting her head back so she could look up into his face. "I don't want you to think that I do this all the time—I don't. I've never had an affair, and even as much as I want you, I'm not convinced I want to walk into one now. I'm not sure I could have you and walk away whole when our nine days is up and the marriage is over. Maybe it would be better if I'd had lots of experience—at least then I would have an answer."

Josh knew with bone-deep certainty that he was glad she hadn't had lots of experience, even though if she had, they might have gotten past kisses by now. The thought of her getting experience with some other man was so unpalatable that he refused to let his mind think about it. Instead, he forced himself to concentrate on her first few sentences.

"I'm not sure that I want an affair, either, honey." He realized with distinct shock that he wasn't sure he could walk away whole if it ended, either. *Not if it ended,* he reminded himself, *when it ended.* Because end it would; there couldn't be a real marriage between them. She was big-city, he was small-town. She was born with a silver spoon, he was not. She was used to a life that included glitzy society parties and trendy cocktail lounges, and he was used to warm family get-togethers and honky-tonk bars. "So I suppose that leaves us with kisses and cold showers." He managed a wry smile and forced his reluctant arms to leave the warmth of her body.

Katherine's mouth drooped in disappointment as she watched him push open his door and round the hood of the car to unlatch hers. He took her hand to draw her out of the Porsche and swung an arm around her shoulders, their hips bumping companionably as they walked silently out of the garage and up the sidewalk to the back of the house. Josh unlocked the door and Katherine stepped in ahead of him, their footfalls loud on the wooden floors until they reached the muffling carpet of the stairs.

What are we going to do about the bedroom? she thought nervously as she walked down the hall.

Josh reached around her to open the bedroom door and she crossed the threshold, refusing to look at him as she moved to the bureau to drop her purse next to his brush and cuff links.

"I'm sleeping on the floor tonight."

His voice was abrupt. Hands tucked into his front jeans pockets, he watched her slender back stiffen and then relax with barely perceptible relief.

"All right."

He didn't look at her as he strode to the head of the bed, pausing to bend and switch on the lamp on the bedside table before he threw back the spread and stripped the top blanket from the mattress. He grabbed one of the pillows and, without uttering a word, stalked to the end of the bed and tossed the summer blanket and pillow down on the floor. Then he left the room.

Katherine sagged against the edge of the bureau when the door closed on his back, listening as the bathroom door clicked open and shut and the soft rush of water told her he was in the shower.

Probably a cold shower, she thought with regret. She stared at the disheveled sheets and blankets for a long moment. How she wished she could share that bed with him. Was she wrong to want some word of reassurance from him that it would be more than a brief affair? She wanted him desperately, and with a sinking heart, she realized that she was already in love with him. If he walked away unscathed and without a backward glance when Cole's wedding was over and their time in Iowa ended, he would take her heart with him. She wasn't sure that she could ever forget him, but she knew with positive clarity that if they made love, she'd never get over losing him.

Damn, she thought with frustration, *why does life have to be so complicated?*

When Josh returned, he found Katherine seated on the edge of the bed, staring unseeingly at his pajama top clutched in her hands.

"Bathroom's free." His words startled her and the gaze she lifted to his was unutterably sad.

"Thank you." Her words were cool and distant, and before he could ask her if she was all right, she brushed past him and was gone.

Oh, hell. He shoved frustrated fingers through his shower-damp hair. *Why does life have to be so damn complicated?*

He switched off the lamp and rolled himself in the light blanket. When Katherine returned, she climbed silently into bed without switching on the light.

"Good night, honey."

His deep voice came quietly through the dark. It shivered up her spine and she clenched her pillow to prevent her arms from reaching out for him.

"Good night."

Josh stacked his hands under his head and lay awake, staring up at the darkened ceiling. The rational part of his brain knew very well that Katherine couldn't feel anything other than a passing physical infatuation for him. Their lives were too different. It was ridiculous to even consider the possibility of turning their sham marriage into a real one. He only wished his unruly heart would listen to his head.

He heard the bedsprings creak as she turned, and it was somehow consoling to know that she was having the same difficulty sleeping that he was suffering. The windup alarm clock on the bedside table ticked loudly, marking off minutes of slow, interminable time that crept at a snail's pace.

Josh glanced at the luminous dial on his wristwatch and groaned. Only a half hour had gone by. He rolled over onto his stomach, clapped the pillow over his head, and slammed his eyelids closed.

The tick of the clock reached him even through the cushion of feathers. Katherine shifted in the bed, tossing and turning, and the springs creaked in a protest that echoed the ticking clock.

Josh endured it for another fifteen minutes.

"The hell with this," he muttered as he threw off the blanket and stood up. Pillow in hand, he stalked around the end of the bed.

"What's wrong?" Katherine sat bolt upright in bed, the sheet clutched to her breasts, her startled gaze taking in Josh's broad-shouldered shape looming over the edge of the mattress.

He threw his pillow down next to hers and she jumped.

"Move over," he growled, and she complied. He lifted the sheet and slid in beside her, leaning up on one elbow to glare down at her. "Look, dammit, neither one of us is getting any sleep. I'm not going to seduce you under my parents' roof. They think you're wonderful and they really believe we're married; when they find out we're not, I'm going to feel like the world's biggest rat. I don't want to add seducing you to my list of things to feel rotten about." He paused to study her reaction. She was watching him with wide, startled eyes, and his voice gentled. "I just want to hold you. I hate to admit it, but I've gotten so used to having you curled up next to me that I can't sleep without you." His fingers gently tucked a strand of hair behind her ear, returning to brush against her cheek before his hand dropped to rest in the center of the scant six inches of white sheet that separated them.

Katherine wanted to throw herself against his chest and weep with relief. He did care. He must. But he clearly didn't want to, because he never once suggested that they consider staying married past their allotted nine days.

"I'm having trouble sleeping without you, too,"

she managed to get out, her throat thick with emotion.

"So you won't mind sharing the bed?"

She smiled, a slow, upward curving of her lips that twisted Josh's heart with a curious, piercing ache. "No," she said softly, "I don't mind."

"Good," he said gruffly. His cheek found the pillow and he curved an arm around her waist, pulling her back against his chest and tucking his legs behind the bend of hers. *Home*, he thought with a deep, unconscious sigh of relief as he buried his face against the thick silk of her hair. *She feels like home and heaven, and everything good I've ever dreamed of or wanted*.

Within minutes, they were both asleep, their bodies pressed together like matching spoons.

The clock ticked on, the night hours wearing away while they slept in peace, until the sun peeked over the eastern horizon and began to climb higher.

Josh drifted slowly upward toward wakefulness. The soft skin beneath his palms and fingertips was an enticement he couldn't resist and, eyes closed, he traced the silky warmth with sleepy pleasure. His mouth tilted in a smile of pure enjoyment as the woman in his arms murmured with sleepy appreciation and snuggled closer.

His fingers traced the inward curve of her waist and slid beneath her shirt to follow the line of her spine upward to her nape before splaying wide to test the silky texture of her shoulder blades and move downward with slow pleasure to her waist.

The pajama shirt was hiked up above her waist, leaving the smooth skin of her abdomen bare to below her navel. Josh trailed his hand across her midriff and belly, brushing the backs of his fingers against the small indentation of her belly button before finding the elasticized waistband of her cotton panties. He frowned sleepily and his fingers instinctively sought the silkier texture of her thigh.

Katherine woke to the slow, hypnotic seduction of a warm male palm caressing her with leisurely, exploring strokes that set her heart pounding and her body reacting in subtle, responsive countermovements to the enticing hands and the warm, hard body she lay against.

Josh's arms contracted, pressing her closer, one hand closing over the back of her thigh to tug it up and over the outside of his.

"Josh," Katherine murmured, her lips parting as she tilted her head back and sought his mouth.

The sound of her voice broke the spell that held them in its grip, halfway between sleep and wakefulness, and they both went completely still. Her lashes flew up and she stared into his heavy-lidded blue eyes, hot with need and a wary shock. His hand curved around the back of her thigh, his fingertips dangerously close to the narrow elastic that stretched the white cotton of her panties beneath her bottom. His thigh was rock-hard where it wedged between hers, and her breasts were softly crushed against his bare chest.

"Oh, my goodness," she whispered softly, her body pulsing with need, demanding satisfaction.

Josh struggled to ignore the heavy pulse of blood that surged through his veins, but there was no way he could hide the effect she had on him. He should let her go and get out of the bed. Now. Before he pushed them both beyond their ability to stop. Even as he thought it, his wayward hand was moving, taking the hem of the pajama top with it as it traveled upward.

Katherine's eyes went lambent, lashes lowering, breath catching as his gaze held hers while the warm, slightly rough skin of his palm and fingertips stroked her feverish skin.

Josh watched the leap of emerald fire in her eyes when his fingers found and brushed the bottom curve of her breast.

"Silk," he muttered hoarsely, "your skin feels like silk and satin."

Katherine was burning up, her heart racing beneath his palm.

"Please," she whispered, twisting beneath his hands, her fingers clenching in the thickness of his hair.

Josh's hand closed gently over the full curve of her breast before his palm brushed lightly over the crest and she gasped, sucking in air with an onslaught of pleasure so intense it approached pain. He saw the heightened sensual reaction that flushed her cheeks and shuddered in the pulse at the base of her throat, and with a groan, he dropped his mouth to take hers.

Katherine tightened her arms around his neck and murmured in satisfaction as he rolled her onto her back and settled over her, his weight a welcome heaviness that blanketed her body.

"Josh." The soft tap of knuckles against the door panel accompanied the purposely lowered voice. "Hey, Josh, you awake?"

Josh's hard body went rigidly still and his head lifted. He squeezed his eyes shut and drew several deep, shuddering breaths before he could open them and speak.

"Yeah, what do you want, Trace?"

"You told me to wake you at five—we're going lake fishing, remember?"

"Dammit," Josh whispered, his voice a mere breath of frustrated sound. "Yeah," he called, loud enough to be heard through the door. "I remember."

"I'll make us a pot of coffee. If you hurry, you'll have time for breakfast before we leave."

"Thanks, Trace. I'll be right down."

The two in the four-poster bed lay perfectly still, listening until Trace's muffled footsteps faded away down the hall and stairs.

Josh closed his eyes and drew a deep breath. When he opened them, he gazed directly into Katherine's emerald eyes and read the same frustrated disappointment that he felt.

"I suppose we should be glad he knocked on the door," he said regretfully.

"I suppose so," Katherine agreed, not sure if she was glad or not.

"Oh, hell," he groaned, and dropped his forehead to rest against hers. "It's damned hard to do the right thing by you when I want you so badly my hands shake."

"They do?" Katherine was a little shaky herself, and immeasurably relieved that he felt the same need that screamed along her nerves.

"Yeah, they do." He grinned wryly. "And that's the least of the reactions that are giving my body fits."

Katherine flushed with color. He didn't have to

detail his other reactions; one very obvious one was solidly wedged against the notch of her thighs.

Josh read her awareness of his condition in the pink that suffused the soft curves of her cheeks and in the lowered sweep of her lashes. "I've got to get out of this bed, honey." He brushed a quick, hard kiss against her softly swollen mouth and levered himself away from her.

Sprawled against the pillows where he left her, Katherine silently watched him collect clothing from the closet. He paused at the door, holding it open to look back at her.

"I'll be back before noon, Katy. If you're not out of this bed by then, I'm joining you, and to hell with good intentions."

And with that, he was gone, the door closing quietly on his broad back.

Maybe I'll sleep the morning away, she thought wistfully. *I'm not sure if I'd mind if he joined me.*

She rolled over and closed her eyes, determinedly wooing sleep.

She was helping Jeannie prepare lunch when he returned.

"I was hoping you'd still be in bed," he whispered as she leaned over his shoulder to set a bowl of vinegar-and-herb-marinated cucumber slices on the table.

"I almost was," she murmured, exchanging a smile of acknowledged kinship with him. They were both fighting to abstain, and it was a battle they were both losing.

Lunch was a boisterous affair. Gavin arrived home from work to join them, and Melanie dropped by in search of Cole and was persuaded to stay for dessert. Katherine was more and more entranced by Josh's family. Their easy camaraderie and close-knit affection were a dramatic contrast to her life as an only child in the calm, organized household in Boston. She'd never really missed having siblings before, but as she watched Josh and Trace trade insults and tease Melanie, she felt a tug of longing to be a part of this clan.

The lunch table held only cake plates and coffee cups when the peal of the front-door bell echoed through the house.

"Now who can that be?" Jeannie asked, glancing at the clock. It was one-thirty in the afternoon, and she wasn't expecting company.

"Don't know, Mom. Want me to answer it?" Trace asked, half rising from his chair.

"No, no, finish your cake. I'll get it." Jeannie rose and hurried out of the dining room on her way through the kitchen to the front hall.

"Well, whoever it is, they're too late for lunch," Gavin commented, shoving back his chair and heading for the kitchen. "Tell your mom I had to get back to work," he said over his shoulder as he disappeared through the door.

"Right, Dad." Trace stood and picked up his cup and empty plate. "I guess I better check in at the shop. I told the guys I'd be back around noon."

"See you tomorrow night," Josh said to his brother's back as he left the room.

"What's tomorrow night?" Katherine asked as she began to scrape crumbs from plates and stack dishes.

"The wedding rehearsal." Josh's blue glance flicked from Katherine's face to Melanie's. "Sure you don't want to back out, Melanie? Cole can be a real pain in the neck."

Melanie laughed and shook her head as she stood. "I love him anyway, and I definitely don't want to back out. I've waited a long time for this wedding." She glanced at her watch and gasped. "Oh, my goodness, I have to run. When you see Cole, would you tell him to call me?"

"Sure," Josh said as she hurried for the back door. His attention turned back to Katherine. "Aha, alone at last." He stood in one swift move and caught her fingers in his. "Come with me, woman."

He tugged her after him, laughing and protesting, into the living room and pulled the double doors shut behind them. A quick glance reassured him that the double doors leading from the living room to the front hall were closed, and he looked back at Katherine, a smile of pure male intent curving his mouth.

"Come here," he said softly.

"No, I don't think so," she said breathlessly. He started to stalk her and she dodged behind a high-backed armchair, laughing. "Josh," she protested, trying to whisper. "Your mother has company!"

He paused, tilting his head toward the hallway door to listen.

"Damn, you're right," he growled in disgust as he heard the murmur of voices. His gaze returned to hers, and warmed as it ran over her pink cheeks and sparkling eyes. "Don't worry, they won't come in here."

No sooner had the words left his mouth than the double doors slid back with a rumble. Jeannie stood in the opening, but it wasn't her slim figure that held Katherine and Josh dumbfounded and silent. It was the woman who stood next to her, her back ramrod-stiff within its pink Chanel suit, her hair gleaming silver beneath a matching pillbox hat, her green eyes swiftly taking in their frozen figures.

"Aunt Addie!" Katherine was the first to find her voice, and she left the protection of the chair's high back to rush across the room and enfold the silver-haired woman in an affectionate hug.

Adelaide Bennington returned Katherine's spontaneous clasp with relief. She'd left Boston determined to get to the bottom of her niece's sudden marriage. The whole family had been stunned by her brief announcement to her father that she was married and leaving Mexico immediately with her husband. It had taken Adelaide a few days to trace Josh McFadden, and although the report held nothing negative to cause concern, still she couldn't rest until she saw for herself that her little chick was truly well and happy.

Her gloved hands patted Katherine's back and then moved to her shoulders to hold her at arm's length. "You look well," she said, her shrewd green gaze moving over Katherine's slim figure in an oversized yellow T-shirt tucked into white short shorts that left the long length of her tanned legs bare. Adelaide's keen eyes didn't fail to notice the pink flush on her cheeks and the happy curve of her mouth.

"I am well, Aunt Addie," Katherine reassured her with a smile, "but what are you doing here? Iowa is a long way from Boston."

"I'm here to meet your young man," Adelaide replied, and dropped her hands from Katherine's shoulders. "Your mother would have come with me, but she slipped on the back deck yesterday and broke her ankle.''

"Oh no!'' Katherine's eyes widened in distress. "Is she all right? She's not alone in the house, is she? Who's taking care of her?''

"She's just fine,'' Addie said, interrupting Katherine's flow of words. "Cousin Mae is with her and will stay until I return—there's absolutely nothing to worry about. The doctor tells us it's only a small bone and in six weeks she'll be out of the cast and spry as ever.''

"Oh, thank goodness,'' Katherine felt the band of worry that squeezed her chest loosen. "You should have stayed with her, Addie.''

"Nonsense,'' Adelaide said bracingly. "One of us had to come to meet your husband. Surely you didn't think you could run off and get married without stirring our curiosity?''

"No, of course not, Aunt.'' Katherine nervously tucked an errant strand of silky hair behind her ear and turned to look over her shoulder. "Josh,'' she said, her voice unconsciously softening with his name. She didn't notice the sharp, assessing glance her aunt gave her, for she was too busy pleading silently with Josh with anxious green eyes. "I want you to meet my great-aunt.''

Josh obeyed Katherine's outflung hand and answered the appeal in her eyes with a reassuring smile as he joined them. He slid an arm around her slim waist and tucked her against his side.

"Aunt Addie, this is Josh. Josh, this is my favorite great-aunt, Adelaide Bennington.''

"I'm pleased to meet you, Miss Bennington.'' Josh gazed into eyes the same emerald shade as

Katherine's. They stared back at him, shrewd, appraising, weighing him with obvious openness. He stared calmly back, refusing to quail before her inspection.

Addie didn't miss Josh's subtly protective, claiming gesture when he caught Katherine's waist and gently pulled her close. It stated quite clearly that Katherine was his. His thick-lashed blue eyes met hers without wavering, unfazed by her imperious gaze. Without embarrassment, she looked him over, head to toe, before she gave an abrupt nod.

"I'm pleased to meet you, too, Josh." She held out a gloved hand and shook his with brisk acceptance. "You'll do, young man." Her gaze snapped to Katherine. "And you, Katherine, I hope you have the good sense to hang onto him. The Benningtons could use some new blood—besides, I suspect he's stubborn enough to handle you. And have lots of children," she added with an abrupt, emphatic nod. "Don't do what your mother did and hatch only one chick. Awful thing to do to a child, raising it without brothers and sisters. Do you agree, young man?" She fixed Josh with a gimlet stare.

"Oh, yes, ma'am." Josh struggled to suppress the grin that tugged at his lips. "I definitely want lots of children."

"Good. I'm getting to be an old lady and I'd like to see Katherine's children before I die." She turned to Katherine. "He's handsome, I'll say that for him. You should have handsome children."

"Yes, Aunt Adelaide," Katherine said solemnly, her eyes dancing with delight.

"Now," Addie said briskly, drawing off her gloves and tucking them into her purse. "I'd like a cup of tea. The food on the flight from Boston was frightful and the tea even worse.''

Jeannie, who had been standing in the hall behind Katherine's great-aunt, hid her smile and stepped forward.

''We've just finished lunch, Miss Bennington, but if you'll come with me, I'll put the kettle back on and we'll have tea in a minute.''

''Good, good. And call me Addie, dear. After all, we're family now.''

Jeannie flashed Josh and Katherine a delighted grin of pure enjoyment and led the erect old lady down the hall toward the kitchen and dining room.

Josh watched them go, feeling slightly stunned. He stared at the empty doorway for a full minute before he looked down at Katherine, who was watching him for a reaction.

''Whew.'' He whistled slowly, an expulsion of breath that reflected his relief. ''So that's your great-aunt.''

She nodded solemnly. ''Yes, that's Aunt Addie.''

''She's quite a character.'' He searched her face. ''You have her eyes, and her cheekbones.''

''So does my mom.'' Katherine eyed him nervously. ''She's a little—eccentric, Josh, but she means well.''

He chuckled, his eyes twinkling. ''Eccentric is an understatement! She's wonderful.''

Katherine relaxed, relieved that he wasn't offended by her great-aunt's blunt inspection.

''She has some good ideas,'' he teased, enjoying the soft feel of her slim curves resting against him. He slid his other arm around her waist and pulled her closer.

"She does?" Katherine narrowed her eyes at him. "Which ones?"

"The one about making babies certainly appeals to me," he drawled, watching the tide of pink move up her cheeks.

"She didn't tell us to make babies, she said she wants to have great-great-nieces and -nephews."

"Same thing. What's the difference?"

"The difference," she said softly as he brushed the tip of her nose with his, "is that you want to practice the *making* part and she wants to see children."

"Well, if you don't practice the *making* part, she won't ever get to see children," he argued logically, tilting his face so his mouth could brush hers.

"Mmmhh." Katherine would have argued, but with his soft, warm lips moving coaxingly against hers, she was having trouble remembering what they were disagreeing about. So she gave up trying to think and closed her eyes, wrapping her arms around his neck and melting against him while he continued to kiss her.

"Ahem."

Josh opened his eyes and glanced up. Cole was leaning against the doorframe, his arms crossed over his chest as if he meant to wait patiently until they were finished. "Go away," Josh mumbled and bent to Katherine. But she evaded him and twisted to look over her shoulder.

"Let me go," she whispered, embarrassed, tugging at his hands.

"All right." He sighed and gave in, allowing her to pull his hands from her waist. "There's too damn many people around here," he grumbled as he watched her hurry from the room. He heard his mother greet her and listened to the subsequent murmur of feminine voices that drifted down the hall before he tore his gaze away from the empty doorway and glared at Cole. "What do you want?" he demanded.

Cole laughed. "It's a little difficult to find privacy in this house, isn't it?"

"Yeah," Josh agreed with a sigh. "Seems like every time I get her to myself, somebody interrupts us."

"Hang in there, Josh. After the wedding, you can take her away to a deserted island somewhere where there won't be anyone to walk in on you."

"Now there's a thought." Josh narrowed his eyes, allowing himself to consider the possibility.

Cole moved away from the door and clapped a commiserating hand on his brother's shoulder. "Why don't you two go out to the folks' lake cabin after the wedding? At least you'll have a few uninterrupted hours there."

"Maybe we will," Josh said noncommittally. He'd thought about the lake cabin. In his inner tug-of-war between wanting Katherine and knowing he shouldn't take her, the knowledge that Gavin and Jeannie's lake cabin stood vacant and with a fully furnished bedroom had teased, tempted, and tormented him unmercifully.

"Josh, guess what?" Katherine interrupted them.

Josh looked up to see her standing in the doorway, eyeing him with equal parts exasperation and amusement.

"What?" He tensed, wondering what else could possibly happen.

"Aunt Adelaide is staying for Cole's wedding. Your mother insisted that she take this opportunity to join in the fun and get to know the whole family better."

Josh stared at her. Her green eyes were flashing what-do-we-do-now signals mixed with helpless laughter. He squeezed his eyes shut and groaned.

"I'll be damned," he said softly, rubbing one hand over his face. "This is getting completely out of hand."

Katherine struggled to control giggles; the look on his face was priceless. And no wonder. Now they not only had to fend off the spontaneous, innocent questions from his family about their *marriage* and courtship, but they had Great-Aunt Adelaide to contend with! She was going to be tougher to fool than all of the McFaddens put together.

"That does it," Josh said with decision, and stalked across the room toward her. He caught her wrist in one hand and didn't even pause, just kept walking on his way out the front door.

"Wait a minute!" Katherine took little running steps to keep pace with his long strides. "Where are we going?"

"To the park." He strode swiftly over the painted boards of the front porch, down the front walk, and, without pausing, turned left to follow the sidewalk.

"What for?"

"To talk."

Katherine planted her feet and stubbornly refused to move. He felt the abrupt tug on his hold and looked back at her, and she glared at him.

"If you don't stop towing me down this sidewalk and tell me why we need to talk, and what about,

I'm going to hit you over the head with the nearest thing I can find." She blew a strand of silky blond hair out of her eyes and frowned at him.

"Sorry." A grin slashed across his face. He knew it wasn't the right time to tell her, but she looked cute as hell standing there threatening him. "I'm taking you to the park, where we can have some privacy and where we can tell each other our life stories and make sure we get our facts straight. Somehow I doubt that any slips we make are going to get past your great-aunt."

"Good idea," Katherine answered promptly, and stepped past him. This time, she was the one tugging on his hand.

"I telephoned my mother," she told him as they walked.

Josh glanced down at her. "How is she?"

"She says she's fine. Addie was right, it was just a small bone." Katherine laughed, her green eyes brimming with mirth as her gaze met his. "She was chasing her little Schnauzer puppy across the deck and he tangled the leash around her ankles. Mom said she fell so fast she hardly knew what happened."

"I'm glad you talked to her," he said. "Do you feel better now?"

"Yes," she said firmly. "Much better."

The city park was only a few blocks away, its oak-dotted grassy expanse sloping down to the lakeshore. Green lake water lapped gently at the strip of sandy beach that was thronged with laughing children and their mothers, and Josh led Katherine along the grassy edge until they had left the noise of the toddlers and their watchful mothers behind.

He dropped down on the grass beneath the spreading branches of a red maple and patted the ground beside him.

"Sit down," he invited. When she complied, folding her legs to sit Indian-style beside him, he leaned up on one elbow, propped his cheek on one fist, and looked up at her. "You first."

"Where do you want me to start?" She gazed down at him, her heart starting its usual slowly increasing thudding when she was close to him. He sprawled lazily on the green grass, his long legs encased in jeans, a plain white cotton T-shirt, with a McFadden Racing Team logo stamped above the pocket, covering his broad chest and leaving the tanned skin of his arms bare below his biceps. Sunshine fingered its way through the leaves of the tree above them and dappled his skin with moving shades of dark and light.

"How about at the beginning?" His slow smile sent ripples of reaction raising goose bumps on her arms.

"All right. I was born in Boston . . ."

The afternoon drifted away while they filled in the gaps. Josh interrupted her to demand more details, fascinated by her description of her life as the only child of doting, amicably divorced parents. Her structured, simple life with her mother and great-aunt in Boston, with its private schools—geared for academia rather than for social status—ballet classes and music lessons, was wildly different from the visits to her father at his home in Bel Air or at any one of the many places around the globe when he was on location. Clearly, however, whether she was with her mother in Boston or her father in more exotic settings, both parents had protected, cherished, and loved her.

"Do you mind that your parents are divorced?" he asked, his curiosity stirred by the descriptions she gave of them.

"Yes, I wish they weren't, especially since I'm very sure that they still love each other."

"They do?" Josh looked shocked. "Then why are they divorced?"

Katherine tugged a blade of grass free and twirled it between her fingers. "I asked my mother that question once, and my father. They both gave me the same answer—in different words, but it meant the same thing. They said that they were complete opposites and that they had nothing in common—they drove each other crazy when they lived together."

"I can relate to that," Josh muttered.

He hadn't planned for her to hear him, but she did. Her fingers tightened and began to carefully shred the green blade of grass into long strips. "Now, some people may think that's a valid theory," she said, her eyes trained on the grass she was slowly but surely demolishing, "but personally, I think it's baloney."

Josh's eyes narrowed. "Why is that?"

"Because I think they chose the coward's way out. You only have to see the two of them in the same room to see the sparks fly—even after twenty years apart. What an appalling waste of two people's lives! Granted, they live productive, satisfactory lives apart, but together . . ." She tossed the mutilated strip of grass down in disgust. "Together, they're magic." She turned her head to look at Josh, her silky hair sliding forward over one shoulder in a blond fall. "Whatever happened to compromise? Whatever happened to loving someone so much that no matter what kind of obstacles existed, two people would stand together and overcome all the roadblocks? Whatever happened to loving someone more than yourself, so that each of you would give a little, out of love for the other person, so that both of you could be happy?"

Josh could hardly breathe. He knew her impassioned plea wasn't about her parents alone. It was about Katherine and Josh.

EIGHT

"I don't know, honey," he said slowly, his troubled gaze meeting hers, "but I do know that sometimes love *doesn't* conquer all. Maybe it wasn't that your father didn't love your mother enough to stay with her. Maybe the real truth was that he loved her enough to let her go."

"Perhaps that's what he thought, but he was wrong. I don't think there's a day that goes by that she doesn't miss him—and he still owns her heart, so she never seriously looks at another man. It's not as if she could fall in love with someone else and build a new life without Daddy."

Was she trying to tell him she wanted a life with him? That for her, too, there would be no sharing of her life with someone else?

"What about your father? Does he feel the same way?"

"I think so—he never remarried. As far as I know, he's never even lived with another woman since

159

Mother.'' Katherine knew Josh was unconvinced. His eyes narrowed as he considered her words. Although neither of them had acknowledged the fact, she was sure he was aware that she was talking about more than her mother and father. She knew that he had decided that there could be no future for them because of their disparate backgrounds, but she felt strongly that he was wrong. ''What I think is so sad,'' she went on, her gaze searching his, ''is that they never gave their love a chance, so they'll never know if they could have made it.''

For one brief, wonderful moment Josh let himself believe that she might be right. But then reality intruded and he pushed the tempting thought aside.

''Yeah, well, I guess we'll never know.'' He stood in one lithe move, and glanced upward through the leafy tree limbs at the westering sun and behind them at the deserted park before looking back down at her. ''We better head back, it's nearly dinnertime.''

Katherine swallowed her disappointment and took his hand, allowing him to pull her to her feet. They retraced their steps through the park and back to the house, both wrapped in their own thoughts, scrupulously maintaining a distance between their bodies.

Katherine flicked a sideways glance at Josh. The black tuxedo fit him like a glove, smoothing over his broad shoulders without a wrinkle, and the formal white shirt made his skin appear even darker. Her heartbeat accelerated and the interior of the Porsche seemed to shrink; she sighed, forcing her gaze away from him and out the side window.

''Something wrong?'' Josh heard the small sound of her sigh as he braked for a stop sign. The powerful engine purred as it idled and Josh took the opportunity to turn his attention away from traffic to the woman beside him.

"No." She turned away from the window to look at him and her hair shifted, barely brushing her collarbone as it slid smoothly over her shoulder. The neat little pale green linen suit she wore had a short, straight skirt. The jacket was tailored to fit close to her body, and a row of crystal emerald buttons marched from the scoop neckline to the hem that flared just below her waist. A tiny hat of the same pale green sat atop her blond hair, its veil covering her face to her cheekbones, turning her eyes into mysterious, emerald green pools. "Nothing's wrong. Should there be?"

"No," he answered abruptly, and tore his gaze away from her to stare out the windshield. He shifted into first gear and the Porsche moved smoothly away from the stop. *Hell, no,* he thought with self-derision, *what could be wrong?* Four days ago in the park, Katherine had all but offered herself to him, and like an idiot, he'd been noble and turned her down. They'd spent the past four days—and nights—treating each other with scrupulous politeness. It was driving him crazy! He was about ready to tell her that if she was brave enough to gamble that they could make it together despite the obstacles, he'd try his damnedest to make her happy.

They reached Grace Lutheran Church and pulled into the paved parking lot without either of them saying another word. Josh handed her out of the car and silently offered his arm. Katherine slipped her gloved fingers into the crook of his elbow, but that was the only part of their bodies that touched as they crossed the lot and climbed the steps to the brick building's heavy double front doors.

"Katherine." Josh halted her on the top step, the fingers of his free hand capturing hers against his sleeve. She looked up at him, and his heart clenched at the thought that this might be the last day he had to spend with her. "I . . ." The door in front of them burst open and two teenagers dashed out, nearly colliding with them. Josh glared at them and they slowed guiltily.

"Sorry, sir," the two chorused, and clattered on down the steps.

"Katherine, there's something I . . ."

A car pulled up to the steps and Jeannie and Great-Aunt Adelaide climbed out.

"Josh—the very person I wanted to find!" Jeannie caught sight of the two poised at the top of the steps and hurried upward. "Would you seat Katherine and Adelaide in the family pew and then find Trace? I promised Melanie that I would bring the guest book and I can't find it anywhere! I think I may have asked Lily to take charge of it—I certainly hope so!"

Josh gave Katherine a helpless look of apology and was relieved to see understanding and acceptance on her face. "Sure, Mom, don't worry. I'll take care of it."

He held open the heavy wooden door for the three women and they entered the church, Jeannie disappearing almost immediately through a door to the left and leaving Josh to escort Katherine and Adelaide to their seats inside the sanctuary.

The church was already half full of wedding guests. Josh ushered the two women, one on each arm, down the crimson carpeting that covered the aisle to the front of the church. He tightened his arm to catch Katherine's hand against his ribs and detain her while he waited for Adelaide to take her seat.

"I'll be tied up for the next few hours until after the ceremony is over and the pictures are taken, but I want to talk to you, alone, without my family surrounding us, at the reception," he whispered in her ear.

"All right," she said softly, rewarding him with a brilliant smile. Hope surged as he squeezed her fingers, then waited until she was seated before he left them. Her loving gaze followed his broad back as he retreated up the aisle, pausing to quietly greet friends and relatives. *Please, God,* she prayed silently, *let him want the same thing I do—a real marriage with love and children and staying together forever, no matter what obstacles we have to overcome.*

"That young woman Cole is marrying has done an excellent job of decorating the church," Adelaide said in a whisper.

Katherine had been so absorbed in Josh that she hadn't paid any attention to her surroundings. Now she glanced around the church and realized that Melanie had indeed done a beautiful job of decorating. White satin bows marked the ends of the oak pews with their red cushions, and matching, smaller ribbons trailed from the huge baskets of summer flowers that stood on each side of the altar. The crimson of the roses tucked among the other blooms in the bouquets echoed the carpet that covered the center aisle of the church and flowed up the three shallow steps to the altar.

"Melanie told me that she's arranged dozens of

weddings, including Sarah's and Lily's, but there was something magical about planning her own," Katherine commented in a hushed voice.

Adelaide's keen eyes surveyed her niece's wistful face as she gazed at the traditional trappings of the church.

"Did you and Josh get married in a church?" she asked with sudden perception.

"No." Katherine's face lit with humor as she remembered the Mexican police chief twirling the keys to the jail cell and the motley group of wedding guests. "It was more of a civil ceremony, although we said our vows before a priest."

"A priest?" Adelaide's strong-boned features reflected confusion. "But you're not Catholic—and neither is Joshua. And how could it have been a civil ceremony if you had a man of the cloth officiating?"

"It's a long story, Aunt Addie. I'll have to tell you about it sometime."

"Yes," Adelaide agreed, nodding her head decisively, "you shall." She scanned the soft, reminiscent smile that curved Katherine's mouth. "Do you regret not having a traditional church wedding?"

Katherine thought about the question for a moment before answering. "No, I truly don't." And she didn't, she realized with surprise. The pomp and ceremony she'd always assumed would accompany a Bennington wedding had been completely missing from the vows that bound her to Josh. But the unorthodox wedding had been the first of the many succeeding adventures that had altered the set, regulated course of her life. "The only thing I regret," she said slowly, "is that we didn't kneel in front of an altar and ask God's blessing on our union. I wish we had done that.''

"You can still do that," Adelaide said bracingly. "Many couples that elope have a blessing ceremony in the church later. There's no reason why you and Josh can't do the same.''

"Hmm," Katherine murmured absently. No reason, except that they were probably going to be filing for divorce. *Unless that's what he wants to talk to me about. Maybe he doesn't want a divorce, either.* She clutched the hope to her heart.

She glanced around the sanctuary. While she and Adelaide had been whispering, the church had filled almost to capacity. The soft background of organ music competed with the low murmur and hushed laughter of friends and family greeting one another. The scent of summer flowers blended with the floral perfumes of women dressed in their Sunday best and the spicy after-shave worn by men in suits and ties.

A fresh-faced young man in a tuxedo ushered Cole's mother down the aisle, Gavin following close behind them. Katherine and Adelaide slid over to make room for them, and Jeannie sat next to her daughter-in-law, smiling her thanks at the young man as Gavin entered the pew.

"Melanie is such a beautiful bride," she whispered, tears sparkling in her gray eyes as she smiled mistily at Katherine.

Impulsively, Katherine reached over and patted Jeannie's hand and was rewarded by the quick, affectionate clasp of her fingers in return. A door set into the wall to their right opened, and the minister, in a white surplice over his black robe and with a leather-covered Bible in his hand, stepped through, followed by Cole, Trace, Jesse, and Josh. Katherine's heart swelled with emotion as Josh's gaze caught hers and he smiled.

"They're certainly a handsome bunch of men," Great-Aunt Addie's voice whispered in her ear.

"Yes, they are, aren't they?" Katherine murmured back, her gaze riveted on the men as they filed past. They made a striking quartet in their formal wear, the McFaddens with their unmistakably Scandinavian, high cheekbones, blue eyes, and blond hair only accented by Jesse's ebony hair and emerald eyes, all of them broad-shouldered and nearly equal in height. Pastor Larson climbed the three shallow steps to the altar and turned to face the sanctuary and the four men in their black tuxedos lined up below him on his left.

The organ music suddenly swelled, moving into the opening strains of the wedding march, and the crowd stood, turning to face the back of the church. Katherine followed suit, but she could feel Josh's gaze like a warm weight against her shoulder blades.

The flower girl stepped through the wide doorway to the vestibule, the hem of her lace-trimmed, rose-colored gown brushing the plush carpet as she walked, scattering rose petals from the basket over her arm. Behind her came the bridesmaids, each of the three wearing ballet-length gowns in varying shades of rose from pale to deepest pink, the crowns of their natural straw hats circled with a garland of summer roses.

At last the bride stepped through the door. Her ivory organza gown with insets of beaded lace was exquisite, the veil a simple gauzy backdrop to her ebony hair. But the glow of love and happiness on her face as her father escorted her to the altar where Cole waited outshone the beautiful dress and all the trappings.

Tears stung Katherine's eyes as Melanie reached the altar and Cole stepped forward to take her hand from her father. She sniffed to keep the moisture from overflowing and felt Adelaide's hand nudge hers to unceremoniously tuck a tissue into her palm. She nodded a silent thank-you and dabbed at her eyes before focusing on the tableau at the altar once again.

"Good afternoon." Pastor Larson smiled at the couple in front of him and at the congregation beyond. "Please be seated."

He waited until the sounds of shuffling feet and rustling clothing had quieted before he opened his Bible.

"Dearly beloved," Pastor Larson began, his deep, melodic tones giving the timeworn words new meaning, "we are gathered here to join together this man and this woman in Holy Matrimony . . ."

Katherine's gaze left Cole and Melanie and moved compulsively to Josh. He was watching her, his deep blue eyes turbulent with an emotion that she couldn't define.

Josh read the emotions that moved across Katherine's face as she watched Melanie kneel beside Cole at the altar, and the need to hold her almost overpowered him. It was all he could do to stay where he was and not cross the short space that separated them and hold her close. He steeled himself to concentrate on the ceremony and keep a lid clamped on his roiling emotions until he could get her alone.

Katherine sipped champagne from a stemmed glass and unobtrusively kept a watchful eye on the entry door of the LakeShore Supper Club. The bridal party had yet to arrive, for the photographer had kept them at the church after the ceremony ended. Katherine would have gladly stayed behind and waited to drive to the reception with Josh, but Adelaide preferred to go straight to the club, and Katherine had agreed. Now she watched the door and impatiently willed Josh to walk through it.

It's been forty-five minutes, she thought, noting the time on the delicate, diamond-studded platinum wristwatch she wore. *How long can it take to snap a few pictures? The sun's already setting, for heaven's sakes!*

Another ten minutes dragged by. Katherine had her back to the door, pretending to listen attentively to a young matron expound on the lack of leadership qualities of CastleRock's Republican mayor, when the McFaddens arrived. The exuberant noise they made as they entered the club was eclipsed by the cheers of welcome and applause from the waiting wedding guests who surged forward to greet them.

Josh's blue gaze searched the jostling crowd for Katherine and found her across the room near the small bar. She stood motionless, a crystal stemmed glass clutched in her fingers, her eyes huge and dark as his gaze found hers.

Katherine's throat went dry when she saw him; her heart ceased beating, only to slam into motion with a force that sent it shuddering against her rib cage when he moved, pushing his way through the crowd toward her. His gaze never left hers until, at last, he reached her.

"Hi," he said softly.

"Hi," she whispered back, her gaze helplessly tracing the beloved planes of his face.

Josh read the yearning on her vulnerable features and without a word took the glass from her hand and set it on the bar. His gaze flicked impatiently over the immediate area and found the exit door that led to a back hall. Threading his fingers through hers, he tugged her after him through the door.

Katherine didn't know where he was taking her. She didn't care. They stepped through the door and into a dimly lit hallway beyond, and Josh crowded her gently against the wall, his mouth dropping to take hers in a long, searching kiss that tried to satisfy all the longings pent-up from the two days he'd just spent without touching her.

It didn't work; it wasn't enough. He broke the seal of their mouths and angled his head in the opposite direction, nibbling at the soft, swollen curve of her lips while his arms wrapped her tighter against him. She was soft and malleable in his arms, pressing against him with an almost frantic need that echoed the desire that clawed and tore at him.

"Katy," he murmured hoarsely, forcing his lips to lift from hers so he could speak. "I don't want a divorce."

Tears welled in her eyes, her arms closing even tighter around his hard body. Katherine struggled to force words past a throat clogged with emotion. "Neither do I," she whispered. "Oh, Josh, neither do I!"

"I'm scared to death of failing you, honey. Our lives have been so different—and a future with me won't be anything like what you could have if you married someone from your own world." He forced himself to say the words his conscience told him he must. "I want you to think long and hard about the changes in your life and what it will mean to marry an ordinary guy like me before you say yes."

"An ordinary guy like you?" Katherine's slow smile lit her face with misty brilliance. "You silly man, whatever makes you think you're ordinary?" She lifted her mouth the tiny distance needed to reach his and gave him her answer without words.

It was long moments later before the growing noise in the big room beyond the isolation of the little hall penetrated their consciousness. Josh reluctantly released her and stepped back.

"I suppose we better join the others before someone comes looking for us." His hands cupped her shoulders, unable to completely break contact with her. He frowned and lifted a hand to cradle her cheek, gently rubbing the pad of his thumb over her lower lip. "I kissed away all your lipstick."

She laughed shakily and touched her fingers to her hat and veil. "Is my hat still straight?"

"Sort of." Josh watched her run smoothing fingers over her hair, feeling an odd peace settle over him. His blood still ran hot and impatient, but the sense of dread and urgency, the feeling that time was running out for them that had strung his nerves taut over the past few days, was gone. In its place was an anticipation that had his body humming with barely controlled desire. Katherine found a compact and lipstick in the tiny shoulder purse she carried and reapplied color to her lips while he leaned a shoulder against the wall and watched her with fascination. "How do you feel about spending tonight away from my family?"

Startled, Katherine looked up from the tiny mirror and straight into Josh's eyes.

"I want you, Katy. My parents have a lake cabin on the east shore of Spirit Lake; we can be alone, without family knocking on doors to interrupt us. Will you come with me tonight?"

He'd told her he wouldn't seduce her. If she went with him, she was making a conscious decision to commit herself to their marriage. She read the knowledge of what he was asking in his eyes, but she had made her choice long before he had asked.

"Yes," she said softly, her heart melting at the relief that was quickly followed by the flare of heat in his blue eyes. "I want you, too, Josh."

He reached for her but stopped himself with iron control just before he crushed her against him. "If I kiss you again, I'm afraid I won't be able to let you go," he said ruefully, his voice gravelly from the effort it took to speak. "We better join the folks outside."

"Am I decent? Is everything back in place?" Katherine asked, turning slowly in front of him.

"Yeah." He straightened the green veil with his fingertip, adjusting it a fraction of an inch lower where it brushed against her cheekbone. "Everything's perfect."

She read the heated appreciation in his blue gaze as it ran over her slim curves before moving back to meet her eyes, and she blushed. "Stop that! Behave yourself!" She tried to sound stern, but the underlying laughter ruined the effect.

"I always behave myself." He looked wounded, but a cocky grin curved his mouth. "Well, not always," he murmured as he smoothed a palm over the curve of her hip before he took her arm and pulled open the door.

A wave of sound greeted them and they stepped into the room without being noticed. Josh halted her at the bar to pick up champagne-filled glasses before sliding a possessive arm around her waist.

"There's Great-Aunt Adelaide, who is . . ." Katherine tilted her head back to look up at Josh; he bent closer to hear her, and the scents of after-shave and pure male that were distinctly Josh flooded her senses. For a moment, her head spun and she completely lost track of what she was going to ask him.

"Hmm?" Josh's glance flicked away from the soft swell of her breasts beneath the green suit jacket and moved upward. The faintly stunned awareness that lurked in the depths of her eyes stole his breath, and his fingers tightened with almost punishing force against her waist.

The sudden pressure snapped Katherine back to awareness and she tore her glance away from his and straightened her body, which had instinctively, unconsciously, softened to lean into his. A quick glance from beneath the shield of her lashes told her that the brief moment had gone unnoticed by the crowd that surrounded them. She searched her memory—what was she going to ask him? *Oh, yes.*

"Who is the man talking to Great-Aunt Addie?" she asked.

"Where?"

"Over near the windows."

Josh's gaze followed the direction of the champagne glass she waved toward the French doors that stood open to a long deck overlooking the lake. He found Great-Aunt Adelaide's erect figure and moved to the man beside her. A grin broke across his face as he recognized the tall, spare body with its shock of snow-white hair.

"That's my uncle Nathan—great-uncle, actually." His eyes narrowed over the two before he glanced down at Katherine. "They make a striking couple, don't they? What do you think—maybe we can play matchmaker and fix your great-aunt up with my great-uncle."

Katherine's own eyes narrowed inspectingly over the still-handsome elder McFadden. He was listening attentively to Adelaide, his gaze focused intently on her face beneath her flower-crowned, wide-brimmed hat. Katherine's gaze moved to her great-aunt and she blinked in surprise. Addie's face was animated and flushed with color, her eyes sparkling as she chatted with Nathan.

"My goodness," Katherine breathed, her eyes wide as she looked back at Josh. "I've never seen my great-aunt talk to a man like that—why, she's almost flirting!"

Josh laughed outright. "It's the McFadden charm—or the Bennington charm. To tell you the truth, I've never seen Uncle Nathan look at a woman quite like that before, either."

"Maybe there's something in the CastleRock water," Katherine commented, shaking her head in amazement as she looked back at the couple near the window.

"Josh McFadden!"

The deep male voice sounded behind them and Josh looked over his shoulder, a grin again breaking over his face. "Mark! How are you?" His hand left

Katherine's waist to clasp the other man's in a warm grip.

"Fine, fine, and yourself?"

"Great, couldn't be better. Katherine"—Josh slung an arm around her shoulders and pulled her forward—"I want you to meet a friend of mine— this is Mark Daly, we went to high school together. Mark, this is my wife, Katherine."

The pleasant smile on the burly man's handsome face turned into a wide grin, delighted surprise reflected in his brown eyes. "This is a pleasure, Katherine." He caught her hand in a warm grip and released her to clap a congratulatory palm against Josh's shoulder. "I'll be damned, Joshua. I never expected you to get married before I did, if ever! And she's beautiful!"

Josh laughed, his eyes crinkling at the corners as he grinned at his boyhood friend. "I suppose that means you thought I'd marry an ugly woman?"

"Hell, no! You know better than that." He winked at Katherine. "He always did have great taste in women, and I can see he still does."

"Thank you." Katherine instinctively liked Mark, and the undisguised approval in his eyes was heartwarming.

"Josh?" Sarah touched his shoulder and claimed the trio's attention. "I want to steal Katherine for a few minutes and introduce her to the Stewarts."

"All right."

Josh's reluctance was plain, and Sarah and Mark exchanged knowing grins before she led Katherine away.

The two men stood side by side, watching as Sarah led Katherine through the crowd.

"She's a beautiful woman, Josh," Mark said.

"Yeah," Josh agreed, "and not just on the outside."

Mark's keen gaze searched Josh's features while he stared at the lovely blonde in the green suit and hat, and his own face softened. "I don't have to ask if you're in love with her. I can tell by the look on your face."

Josh shrugged, a little uncomfortable that his thoughts were so easy to read. "I won't deny it, Mark."

"Are you two planning a family?" Mark asked, sipping champagne.

"Sure, I suppose so." The thought of having children with Katherine made his heart ache with sudden longing.

"You ought to move back to CastleRock, Josh. It's a good place to raise kids. Not to mention how happy it would make your folks to have you and your family close."

"My mom would be over the moon," Josh said dryly, his mouth quirking in a grin.

"So would I. If you settled here, maybe I'd finally stand a chance of convincing you to go to work with me."

"We have this conversation every time I see you, Mark," Josh said, drawing his gaze away from Katherine to focus on his friend.

"Damned right we do." Mark nodded his head abruptly. "And we'll keep having it until you agree to come to work on the force. Now, don't argue with me." He raised a hand, palm outward, to forestall a refusal from Josh. "I know that the CastleRock Police Department can't offer you the sophistication of the federal Department of Immigration, nor would you have the prospect of traveling and seeing more of the world. But it's a good place to work, and do you really want to keep traveling around for months on end when you have a wife and maybe kids at home waiting for you?''

Josh was silenced by his logic. Mark was right. Now that he had Katherine to consider, moving back to CastleRock didn't sound like such a bad idea. After all, he reminded himself, it wasn't as if he'd never thought about returning to CastleRock. It was just that in the past, settling down in CastleRock was always something he planned to do in the far-off, distant future. Suddenly, the future didn't seem so distant and the prospect of traveling to strange places only made him feel weary.

"You may be right, Mark," he said slowly.

"What?" Mark sputtered and nearly choked on a mouthful of champagne. "You mean you're willing to consider working with me?"

"Yeah, maybe." Josh watched Mark brush droplets of sparkling wine from his linen suit coat and grinned. "Don't act so shocked, Mark. A man might think that you never really expected me to agree with you. Didn't you think I'd give in eventually?"

Mark shrugged, his broad shoulders moving beneath the dove-gray linen. "Hell, I don't know. You've been saying no for so many years that I suppose I'm programmed to keep arguing—you sort of took the wind out of my sails by saying *maybe*."

Music from the three-piece band interrupted them, and they watched as Cole led Melanie out onto the polished floor. He took her in his arms and they hesitated, waiting for the beat, before he swept her into the graceful, romantic steps of a waltz.

"You know," Mark said reflectively, "there's something about weddings that makes a man wish he had a bride of his own. You know what I mean, Josh? Josh?"

But Josh didn't hear him. He was wending his way purposefully through the crowd toward Katherine.

Mark grinned and shook his head. "You'd think it was his wedding night instead of Cole's."

NINE

"Excuse me, ladies." Josh's deep tones behind her interrupted Meg Stewart as she chatted with Sarah and Katherine, and all three women looked over their shoulders at him. "Sorry to break in like this, but I want to steal Katherine away."

Meg gazed fondly at Jeannie and Gavin's youngest son. "We'll let you take her only if you promise to bring her back."

"I promise," Josh lied glibly, his gaze flicking to Katherine. *Of course, I'm not saying when,* he thought, without a twinge of remorse.

"It was nice meeting you, Meg," Katherine said with sincerity and managed a quick good-bye as Josh deftly maneuvered her away from Sarah and Meg. With the same measure of easy diplomacy, he kept her moving and avoided the friends who would have stopped them to say hello as he led her onto the small dance floor.

"At last," he murmured against her temple. "How long do we have to stay here?"

Katherine luxuriated in the snug fit of his arms around her. "I don't know," she whispered back, her lips brushing the lobe of his ear, "but I don't want to offend Melanie and Cole by leaving too early."

"Offend Cole and Melanie?" Josh searched the crowd of dancers until he found the newly wedded couple. "From the look on their faces, I'd say you could drop an atom bomb on this reception and they wouldn't even know it."

"Well," she murmured, anticipation bubbling through her veins, "then I guess it doesn't matter when we leave, does it? Except that Sarah asked if I would help pass out the little packets of rice to the guests to throw at the bride and groom when they leave."

Josh lifted his head a fraction of an inch so he could see her face. "Damn." His deep groan reflected his reluctant acceptance. "I suppose you'd object if I tossed you over my shoulder and carried you out of here?"

She laughed and smoothed her fingertips against the warm skin of his nape just above his shirt collar, her gaze lovingly tracing his disgruntled features. "I think that might be just the tiniest bit extreme."

"I feel extreme," he growled, impatient to get her alone. "But I'll behave myself—only until Cole and Melanie leave, though. If Sarah thinks of one more thing for either of us to do, I'll dump her in the punch bowl."

An hour passed before the bride and groom were ready to leave. That hour turned out to be a long sixty minutes for Josh. No sooner would he get Katherine to himself on the dance floor than an old high school friend, or a relative, would break in and claim her, or both of them, for a dance or a drink. He endured it as stoically as possible, with as much grace as he could muster.

Finally and at last, it was time for Melanie to toss her bridal bouquet. Josh held Katherine in front of him in the midst of the laughing crowd, his hands resting on her narrow waist, and he dropped his head to nuzzle her cheek.

"If one more person tells us that we look as starry-eyed and romantic as Cole and Melanie and they can't tell which of us are the newlyweds, I'm going to tell them the truth," he whispered in her ear.

Katherine turned her head, her amused green eyes only inches from his narrowed blue ones. "And what is the truth?" she murmured back.

"That we *are* newlyweds and tonight is our wedding night, too."

"Oh."

Her eyes darkened to deep emerald and Josh felt a shiver of reaction quiver through her slim form where it rested against him. He slid his arms around her waist to hug her closer and bent to brush a kiss against the bare skin of her shoulder. "Cole can't be any more impatient than I am," he said softly as he lifted his head, whispering so that only she could hear.

Katherine couldn't answer, her breath snatched away by the naked need written across his face. Heavy-lidded, his eyes were dark with wanting that was an echo of the need that hummed through her own veins.

"There she is!"

"Throw it to me, Melanie!"

The laughing shouts of the semicircle of single girls and women shattered the web of intimacy that surrounded them and Josh tensed, ruthlessly tamping down his need to carry her off.

"Soon," he murmured, taking one last, searing glance at her helplessly vulnerable face before forcing his gaze away from her.

Katherine watched his expression, the naked longing smoothing away to polite interest as he switched his gaze to Melanie's laughing face. His arms at her waist kept her chained against him, and she struggled with her own emotions in an attempt to present a calm face to the world.

She laughed and clapped with the rest of the crowd as Meg's daughter, Kari, caught the bouquet with blushing embarrassment. The crowd surged after Cole and Melanie as they left the LakeShore, pelting them with rice as they dashed to their waiting car.

The turquoise-and-white '59 Thunderbird that stood at the curb had tin cans and old shoes tied to the bumper, and pink-and-white paper streamers were tied to every possible knob and handle on the classic car.

"Why aren't they taking Cole's Porsche?" Katherine asked Josh with curiosity.

"Because Dad's T-bird has sentimental meaning for them." Josh shrugged at her inquiring glance. "I have no idea why—and I didn't ask." He glanced around them and unobtrusively tugged her to the back of the crowd.

"What are you doing?" she asked as he hustled her through the door and across the deserted supper club to the little hallway beyond.

"I'm kidnapping you while they're all busy outside.'' He threaded his fingers through hers, fitting his callused palm against the soft warmth of hers, and pushed open the door beneath the neon exit sign at the end of the hall.

Katherine blinked as they left the relative dimness of the hallway for the fading sunlight outside. The back exit let out into the LakeShore's paved parking lot and Josh led her through the rows of parked cars to the Porsche, where he unlocked the doors and handed her in without speaking.

The driver's side door closed with a solid sound, enclosing them in the leather-scented interior of the sports car. Josh turned his head, his hot blue gaze snaring hers.

"Come here," he said softly, and reached for her.

She went willingly and he wrapped his arms around her, breathing in the scents of perfume and warm woman just before his mouth found hers. Long minutes later, he forced himself to release her, brushing her mouth with his one last, lingering time.

"The cabin's only fifteen minutes from here," he said huskily, a wry, self-mocking grin curving his mouth, "but if we don't leave now, I'm never gonna make it."

"Fifteen minutes isn't so long," Katherine said dreamily, resting her cheek against the supple leather of her seat as she turned her head to watch him start the car.

"No?" He quirked an eyebrow as he reversed the car out of its parking space, shifting into first to weave their way out of the lot. "It's fifteen minutes *too* long as far as I'm concerned." He glanced both ways before pulling out into the street. "Fasten your seat belt, honey; maybe it won't take us fifteen minutes after all.''

Ten minutes later, Josh slowed and turned off the highway into a narrow, graveled lane. Ahead of them, the lake surface glistened beneath a quarter moon, and a small cabin sat beneath the trees, its windows dark.

''I cut five minutes off the record time,'' Josh commented with satisfaction as he parked the car and led Katherine up the brick walk to the narrow porch.

''You drove like a maniac,'' she scolded him. The adrenaline generated by their race along the lakeshore road still pumped through her veins. ''Thank goodness there weren't any police around, or you would have gotten a speeding ticket that would have rivaled the national debt!''

Josh grinned as he unlocked the door and pocketed the key. ''Hell, honey, the cops would have thought it was Cole driving and wouldn't even have bothered to follow me.''

''That's no excuse!'' she sputtered and gasped, catching her breath as he bent and slipped an arm behind her knees and the other around her shoulders, swinging her off her feet to cradle her in his arms. She went silent, her laughter fading as all amusement disappeared from his face, replaced by an aching intensity that riveted her.

''I'm sorry if I scared you, Katy, but I just couldn't wait any longer.''

Under the shadowy overhang of the porch, his face was mysterious dark planes and angles, his blue eyes hot beneath half-lowered lashes. The nervous butterflies that had fluttered their frantic wings in her midriff ever since they left the LakeShore faded away, and she reached to trace the hard bones of his cheek and jaw with her fingertips.

"I'm not afraid, Josh," she whispered, absolutely sure at this moment that their love was right.

Josh pushed open the door and carried her over the threshold, kicking it shut behind them with unerring accuracy as he bent his head to close the space between her mouth and his. His long strides ate up the distance across the darkened living room to the bedroom, stopping at the edge of the bed. Now that he had her safely alone, with no one to interrupt them, some of the urgency drained away, leaving only the overwhelming need to make the most of their time together.

He freed her legs, almost groaning aloud with the sheer pleasure that gripped him at the slow slide of her body down his as he set her on her feet.

"I can hardly believe I have you all to myself," he murmured, his voice rough with emotion as he cupped her cheek to smooth his thumb over the soft skin. "No one to knock on our door—just you and me."

Katherine's mouth curved upward in a smile that trembled and he brushed the pad of his thumb against her bottom lip. Her lashes lowered to half conceal her eyes, and her body melted against his. His mouth replaced his thumb and her mouth opened beneath his, welcoming the surge of his tongue into the sleek wetness. Josh's arms tightened and Katherine's arms clung to his neck as she went up on her toes to pull him closer. The movement tugged the bottom of her jacket upward and out from under Josh's hand, leaving a strip of bare skin between it and the waistband of her skirt.

The soft material shifted out from beneath his hand, leaving his palm and fingertips resting against the silky warmth of Katherine's bare skin. His fingers moved with compulsive fascination against her waist, brushing rhythmically, but the close-fitting jacket fitted so snugly that he couldn't push his hands beneath it.

Katherine, awash in a sea of sensation, vaguely knew when his hand moved between them and slipped the crystal buttons free, and she groaned with sheer pleasure when he flattened his palm against her bare midriff before stroking upward in a caress that ended when his hand closed over the swell of her breast.

Josh lifted his head and looked down at her. Her head lay against his shoulder, her face tilted back to look up at him through drowsy eyes. Arousal flushed the soft skin of her face, her mouth red and softly swollen from the pressure of his. His gaze moved lower, drifting over her throat and fragile collarbones. The edges of her unbuttoned jacket still overlapped to conceal her body, his jacket sleeve disappearing beneath the green linen. He didn't want to leave the soft curve of her breast and the rapid thud of her heartbeat that he could feel beneath, but he wanted to see her. Slowly, he pushed her jacket back.

Katherine stood in his arms, vulnerable and trusting. She knew how much he wanted her. She could feel it in the tenseness of his muscles; she could see it in the flush that streaked his cheekbones and in the heat that lay in his thick-lashed blue eyes. Still, his hands were infinitely gentle, treasuring the vulnerable curve of her breast as they moved to brush back her jacket.

"Katy," he breathed softly, his lashes lifting to reveal blue eyes blazing with need mixed with stunned reverence, "you're so beautiful."

His fingers trembled where they traced the delicate lace-and-satin bra. He bent his head and brushed his lips, warm and cherishing, against the swell of her breast just above the cream lace. Again and again, he kissed her, his mouth worshipping her, and Katherine's hands closed into fists over the material of his tuxedo jacket. Her whole body felt flushed with heat and she barely noticed when he pushed the jacket off her shoulders. It dropped unheeded to the floor at their feet but she didn't care, for his mouth had returned to brushing kisses alternately against the bare skin of her shoulders, throat, and breasts. She moaned and twisted against him, tugging at the studs on his shirtfront, frustrated at her inability to pull them free.

Reluctantly, Josh forced his mouth to desert the soft skin of her throat just below her ear and looked down at her.

"What is it, honey?"

"Your shirt's stuck," she murmured.

Distracted, Josh touched her mouth with his, stopping himself with an effort when he realized that he hadn't answered her. What had she said? Something about his shirt?

He lifted his head and leaned back to look down. Her hands rested against his shirt front. "What's wrong with my shirt?" he asked foggily, trying to concentrate when all he could think of was how soft her skin was beneath his hands.

"It's stuck," she whispered, looking up at him through her lashes. "I want it off—take it off."

He stared at her for a moment while his brain struggled to cope with processing thoughts. He wanted his clothes off, too, but he didn't want to take his hands away from her long enough to do it. Unfortunately, he couldn't think of any other way to accomplish undressing.

"Take my jacket off, first," he said, his voice rusty.

Katherine obeyed, his heartbeat shuddering beneath her fingers as she slid her palms under the lapels and over his shoulders to push the jacket off. Josh's hands continued their small, stroking caresses over her back until he was forced to remove them so she could tug the black tuxedo sleeves down his arms and off. The jacket joined hers on the floor.

Josh didn't bother unbuttoning the black-and-silver studs; instead, he caught the edges of the shirtfront in each hand and ripped them open, shrugging out of the shirt and tossing it behind him with one swift movement. He plunged his hands into her hair and buried his mouth against hers, not even noticing when her little green hat went tumbling to disappear in the shadows of the moonlit room.

Katherine moved into the circle of his arms and he wrapped her against him. His bare chest was silky skin over powerful muscles and she was swamped with an avalanche of sensation. She slid her arms around his neck, the sensitive skin of her wrists and forearms registering the heat and textures of his body. His fingers brushed against her back and he tugged her arms down, leaning away from her long enough to pull the satin bra straps free.

Naked from waist to shoulders, they pressed together, need spiraling as silky softness shifted against muscled hardness. Josh tugged the zipper at the back of her skirt, loosening the green linen so he could push it down over her hips. It pooled around her feet and he dragged his mouth from hers and lifted his head to look down at her. He'd expected to find the plain white cotton panties he'd glimpsed peeking from beneath his pajama shirt in their bedroom, but instead, she wore tiny cream bikinis with a matching garter belt.

"Where . . ." He swallowed, smoothing his palm over the indentation of her waist and the outward curve of her hip. His heavy-lidded gaze swept up to meet hers before returning to follow the movement of his hand as it loitered over the narrow cream satin where it curved over her hip, then followed the lacy edge inward. Her stomach muscles quivered under his exploring fingers and his lashes lifted, his hot blue glance flying to meet hers. "Where did you get these?" he asked rustily, his thumb tracing the dimple of her navel.

The heat in his eyes was as powerfully seductive as his touch and she could hardly breathe under the weight of his stare.

"Melanie," she managed to get out. "She said it was a wedding present from her and Victoria's Garden."

"Remind me to thank her," he whispered. "But how do I get you out of them?"

"There's a hook—in the back."

Josh's heated glance held hers as his hand left her thigh and moved to find the tiny hook and eye at the base of her spine. He maneuvered the hook free with one smooth move and Katherine's eyes narrowed.

"You're awfully good at that," she accused throatily.

"Sheer luck," he growled. "Somebody up there knows I haven't got any patience left." His hands cupped her bottom and caught her against him, shifting her slowly from side to side, teasing them both until the heat they generated threatened to burn them alive.

"Please, Josh," she begged. "I don't have any patience left, either."

"Good," he growled, and caught her against him with one hand while he bent over her to pull back the bedcovers. "I want you to be as insane with wanting as I've been ever since Mexico." He closed his hands over her shoulders and gently pushed her to a seat on the edge of the mattress before he went down on one knee in front of her. Moonlight glinted off the tumbled mass of her hair and stroked the high curve of her bare, rose-tipped breasts with cool light. She leaned toward him and he groaned, pressing a hard kiss against her mouth before breaking away. "If we don't slow down, honey, I'm not even going to get your clothes off."

He smoothed the silk hose down her legs, lingering over the soft exposed skin.

Katherine caught her breath when his hands stroked back up her bare legs, his thumbs brushing the inside of her thighs until they reached the cream lace edge of her bikinis.

"Lie back," he ordered softly, and she obeyed. He slid his thumbs under the tiny strips of lace over her hips and tugged them downward and off.

She should have been embarrassed, Katherine realized hazily, but she only felt a heated surge of delight at the expression of fierce pleasure on his face as he stared at her sprawled against the pillows.

He stood and stripped off the rest of his clothes with swift movements and dropped something from his pocket on the bedside table before joining her. Katherine opened her arms, murmuring with satisfaction when his heavy weight lowered to settle over her.

The soft giving of her warm curves beneath his, the welcome clasp of her arms reaching to press him closer, and the eagerness of her mouth parting beneath his pushed him over the edge.

"I can't wait, sweetheart," he groaned in apology. "Next time," he promised hoarsely as he fumbled for a small, square packet on the bedside table and tore it open with his teeth.

Katherine barely registered his words or his care for her before he settled against her, joining his body with hers with one smooth, heavy thrust. She was too caught up in the magic of his mouth on hers, in the rhythmic dance of passion that whirled her faster and faster until the world exploded around her.

Exhausted, she lay sprawled beneath him, his big body blanketing her own smaller frame, sealed to his with the sheen of dampness generated by the heat that had burned through their bodies.

Josh levered himself up on his elbows and looked down at her. Her face was flushed and drowsy with satisfaction, and his worry and guilty concern that he'd gone too far, too fast, for her loosed their grip. He combed his fingers through her hair, spreading the silky strands against the white cotton of the pillowcase as he searched for the words to tell her what a miracle she was and how much holding and loving her meant to him.

"Katy." His voice was a husky whisper in the silent night, his eyes dark as his gaze stroked over the beloved planes of her face. "I love you—no matter what happens, I want you to remember that I love you."

Katherine's eyes misted with tears, her arms tightening where they circled his lean waist. "I love you, too," she breathed, her voice wobbling as teardrops trembled on her lashes and spilled over to paint damp, silvery trails down her cheeks.

"Don't cry," he said, his hands moving to cradle her face so his thumbs could wipe away the dampness. "I don't ever want you to cry because of me."

"I'm crying because I'm happy, not because I'm sad."

Josh eyed her skeptically, but the brilliant smile that curved her mouth and lit her misty eyes convinced him.

"Women," he muttered with wry acceptance. "I'll never understand women."

"You don't have to understand *women*," she said, sliding one bare foot up the back of his calf, her toes curling in reaction as the soft hair on his leg prickled her sensitive sole. "You just have to understand one woman—me."

"Okay." He bent his head the few brief inches necessary to touch her mouth with his. "I'll try."

"Mmm," she murmured, her mouth curving in a smile of pleasure beneath the brush of warm lips and the exploring roughness of his tongue. "I like the way you try. More, please."

It was nearly dawn before they finally fell asleep, Katherine sprawled contentedly across his chest, his arms around her waist and her knee nudged between his thighs. The long hours had flown by as they alternately confided and explored each other's thoughts between long, satisfying bouts of lovemaking and exploring each other's bodies.

"What the hell is that?" Josh growled with irritation, slitting one eye open to stare up at the ceiling while his brain struggled to grasp what had awakened him.

"Mmm." Katherine yawned and snuggled closer, refusing to open her eyes. "I think it's the telephone."

"The telephone?" Josh frowned, foggily trying to equate the noise he heard with his certain knowledge that there hadn't been a phone in the cabin the last time he was home. "Damn," he agreed reluctantly, "you're right. It's a phone ringing."

He tried to ignore it, but it continued ringing.

"I better answer it, honey." He kissed the top of Katherine's head and she protested sleepily when he shifted her off him and slid out from beneath the sheet. "I'll be back," he promised, shoving his long legs into the black tuxedo slacks and grinning when she half opened her eyes in response.

Katherine stared with open, unabashed appreciation at his broad shoulders, lean waist, and long legs as he left the room, warmth stirring in the pit of her stomach as she stretched, memories of the night before bringing a satisfied, contented smile to her face. She tugged his pillow closer and wrapped her arms around it, breathing in his scent that clung to the white cotton.

From beyond the bedroom, the murmur of his deep voice rose and fell in conversation before silence once again claimed the lake cabin. Katherine waited expectantly for him to return, anticipation slowly heating her blood, her gaze fastened on the doorway. But seconds dragged by, and then minutes, and when he still hadn't returned, she slipped out of bed and paused to pick up his shirt from the floor. She shoved her arms through the sleeves and buttoned it closed as she left the bedroom, padding barefoot into the living room, only to find it empty. Frowning, she scanned the room and located the telephone, its receiver resting securely in the cradle, on a square pine table at the end of a cushioned wicker sofa.

The rushing of tapwater sounded in the quiet house and her gaze flicked to a doorway across the room. Cabinet doors opened and closed with soft, decisive clicks, and Katherine followed the sound to the kitchen. Josh stood with his back to her, measuring coffee grounds into the basket of an electric coffeemaker.

"Josh?"

His shoulders tensed and his hands paused for a moment before he returned to dumping the coffee into the filtered basket. He pushed the switch to "On," snapped the plastic top back on the can of coffee, and slid the can back on the cabinet shelf before he turned to face her.

"Josh, what's wrong?" Sudden fear gripped her when she saw his face. His handsome features were smooth and remote, and she could read nothing in his expression, but her instincts told her the call hadn't been good news. "Who was on the phone? What did they want?"

TEN

"I can't tell you," he said, his voice flat.

"Why?" Her green gaze searched his face in bewilderment. She could hardly equate this unemotional, cool man with the Josh she'd just spent the night with. Gone was the open warmth of the McFaddens' youngest son, and in his place was the hard-eyed, dangerous stranger she'd first met in Mexico.

"I just can't." He leaned one hip against the tiled countertop, his hands stuffed into his pockets. "You better get dressed. I'll take you back to the house; then I have to leave."

"Leave? You're going to leave? Where are you going?"

"Back to Mexico."

"Oh." She stared at him for a long moment before she straightened, visibly collecting herself. "I'll get dressed. It won't take me long to pack and say goodbye to Aunt Addie—"

"No," he said, interrupting her. "I'm going alone, Kate."

The swift hurt that darkened her green eyes stabbed him, and his hands closed into fists to keep from reaching out for her.

"I don't understand, Josh," she said gravely, clasping her hands together in front of her to still their trembling. She needed to hold onto something, for her whole world was suddenly tilting out from under her feet. "If you're going back to Mexico, why can't I go with you?"

"Because I have to go back to take care of some unfinished business. I can't take you with me, it isn't safe."

"Does this have anything to do with the man who knifed you?" The tremors were increasing, shaking her insides. She fought to keep the quivering from affecting her voice.

"I can't tell you, Katy," he repeated. "I warned you, remember? I can't tell you anything about my work."

"Yes," she said, swallowing with difficulty past the lump of fear in her throat, "I remember." She drew a deep breath and forced a wobbly little smile of acceptance. "So how long will you be? Do you want me to wait for you at your parents' home, or should I go back to Boston and pack?"

"No." Josh steeled himself for her reaction. "I don't want you to wait for me and I don't want you to pack. I want you to go through with the divorce."

Katherine was too stunned to speak. Her body and brain felt numbed; even her lashes seemed to fall in slow motion as she blinked in disbelief before they lifted. She purposely forced her eyes to open wider, but the scene didn't change. Josh still stood across the kitchen, leaning against the cabinet, his grim face belying his casual stance.

"I don't believe this," she said softly, almost to herself.

Josh winced inwardly, preparing himself for an explosion of anger from her that he knew he richly deserved. *You should have thought of this before you slept with her*, his conscience berated him. *You knew Castaneda and Mexico were unfinished business. You should have asked her if she was willing to chance becoming a widow before she even had a honeymoon!*

But it was too late for regrets. All he could do was stand stoically and endure the storm of fury that he could see growing on her face.

"You want a divorce?" The numbness that had gripped her at his words was quickly wearing off, burned away by the rage that swept through her. "Would you mind telling me why?"

He'd already decided to tell her only part of the reason for his insistence on following through with his original plan. "Because ever since I met you in Mexico, I've turned your life upside down. I want you to have time to decide if you really want to be married to me—without the influences of weddings, and my family, and my threatening to leave you in a Mexican jail if you don't agree."

Katherine felt a burst of relief that he hadn't said he didn't love her, but it was quickly buried under righteous anger as she realized what he was saying. "You mean you think I'm such an airheaded little twit that I was swept away by all the romanticism and that I'll just forget you once I return to my own normal life?'' Josh opened his mouth to respond, but she didn't give him time. "You think I'm a complete idiot and that last night was just a one-night stand? Is that what you think? Is that all last night meant to you?''

"I didn't say that," he said through his teeth, "and you know I don't feel that way about last night. I just think you need some time and distance to think about us—to get some perspective."

"Humph!" She glared at him, fairly sizzling with fury. "I think one of us needs some perspective, all right, but it's not me!!''

Josh watched her turn on her heel and stalk out of the room.

"Oh, hell!" He glared at the empty doorway, his expression black. The timer on the coffeepot behind him buzzed loudly and he jerked in reflex before switching his irritated glance to the offending coffeemaker. "Shut up," he growled, before yanking open a cupboard door to search for mugs.

An hour later, Katherine followed him out the front door of his parents' house and down the front walk. The Harley leaned on its kickstand at the curb, its sleek black-and-chrome lines no less dangerous-looking than the man at her side. She was vividly aware that his mother and father and her great-aunt stood on the front porch watching them, so she didn't shrug off Josh's arm from around her shoulders. They reached the low-slung bike and halted.

Josh glanced over her head at the trio on the porch and removed his arm from her shoulders, his hands dropping to rest lightly on each side of her waist.

"Thanks for not saying anything in front of my folks," he said gruffly.

"I like your parents. I wouldn't do anything to upset them," she answered, stiffening her body against the seductive pleasure of his hands curved around her waist and the warm enticement of his body only inches from hers. He was dressed in a clean khaki shirt and blue jeans, his favorite black cowboy boots on his feet. He looked good enough to eat and it made her furious that, even angry as she was with him, she still found him irresistibly attractive.

"Yeah, well"—he shrugged—"I appreciate it." He dug into his pocket and extracted a business card. "I almost forgot—this is a phone number where you can reach me in an emergency, or to serve the divorce papers." His intent blue stare was stroking over her face, enabling him to memorize each soft curve, so he knew instantly when her temper flared. He immediately covered her mouth with his fingers. "Don't say it," he ordered softly. "I don't want to argue with you—not now."

"If you don't want an argument, don't start one," she said tartly, her lips moving against the pads of his fingers.

"I don't want to argue." He tucked the card into the scoop neckline of the deep rose cotton suntop she wore, the backs of his fingers lingering to brush against the silky slope of her breast. He glanced down at his hand, slowly withdrawing his fingers before looking up at her. "I want you to kiss me good-bye." He caught her waist and drew her against him.

Katherine's legs, bare beneath white shorts, went weak as he pressed the lower half of her body against his. Furious as she was with him, she still couldn't resist kissing him good-bye.

"All right," she agreed, and slipped her arms around his neck. "But only because our relatives are watching and they might think it odd if we didn't."

"I don't care why you kiss me," he growled, lashes lowering over hot blue eyes as his head bent to hers. "Just do it."

"You're impossible and arrogant and mmph . . ." His mouth found hers, muffling her words.

He kissed her as if it were the last time, as if this would be the only time he'd ever get to hold her again, and all thoughts of anger and protest evaporated from Katherine's consciousness. She melted against him and his arms crushed her closer as his mouth took hers with a fierce desperation that echoed her own.

Josh had to force himself to stop kissing her. His whole body clenched in rejection as his arms left her and he tugged her hands from around his neck.

"I have to go," he said huskily, surprised that his voice actually worked.

He stepped back and away from her. Katherine willed her tears not to fall as he swung his leg over the bike and kick-started it. The powerful machine came to life with a roar, and he leaned it sideways and raised the stand with one booted heel.

Katherine stepped close, her lips brushing his ear as she shouted over the noise of the engine, "Be careful!"

"I will." He turned his head, his blue gaze snaring hers before he caught the back of her head in one palm and tilted her face to his for one last, hard kiss. Then he released her and glanced at the porch, lifting one hand in farewell before the bike moved away from the curb.

Katherine stood in the street, her misty gaze fastened on his broad back as the powerful bike moved easily down the street. But Josh didn't look back, nor did he wave again, and she waited until he leaned into a turn and disappeared at the far end of the block before she went slowly up the walk to the house.

"Don't look so sad. He'll be back before you know it, Katherine," Gavin said sympathetically, the sad droop of her mouth touching his soft heart.

Katherine gave him a halfhearted smile but didn't respond.

Gavin and Jeannie exchanged glances before looking to Adelaide for help.

"Well, now," Addie said bracingly, fixing her niece with a keen emerald stare, "what are you going to do until Joshua returns, Katherine? I'm going back to Boston tomorrow and you can go with me."

Katherine started to nod in agreement, but the plan that had been slowly brewing in the back of her mind suddenly reached the boiling stage, and instead, she shook her head decisively. "No, thank you, Aunt, but I'm not going back to Boston for a while, not until Josh can go with me."

"Oh, then you're staying with us, then." Jeannie smiled with pleasure. "I'm so glad. It will give us all a chance to get to know each other better."

Katherine smiled apologetically at her mother-in-law. "No, Jeannie, I'm afraid I'm not going to stay in CastleRock, either."

"Then where are you going?" Adelaide asked, her gaze narrowing over Katherine's expression of resolve.

"To Mexico." Katherine almost laughed aloud at the confused look on all three faces. "I'm going back to Santa Rosa. I'll stay with Dad while I wait for Josh to finish his business, and then we'll come back together."

"Back where?" Gavin asked. "To CastleRock or Boston? Or to Josh's apartment in Houston?"

"Back here—to CastleRock." Katherine eyed Jeannie mischievously. "Didn't Josh tell you? Mark Daly offered him a job with the CastleRock Police Department and he's thinking seriously of accepting."

"Oh, that's wonderful!" Jeannie's face lit with joy, and Gavin's expansive grin echoed her happiness.

"Yes, isn't it?" Katherine agreed. *Now all I have to do is convince Josh that his life in CastleRock is going to include me and children.*

Katherine waited three days in Santa Rosa before her patience ran out. When she dialed the number on the business card Josh had given her, she reached an office in Houston, but he wasn't there.

"I know he's not in the office," she said patiently. "He's in Mexico. I want a forwarding number in Santa Rosa where I can reach him."

"I'm sorry, ma'am," the secretary advised her, "but that information is not available. I'm not authorized to give out a forwarding number."

"Then let me speak with someone who is," Katherine insisted.

"Very well. Just a moment, I'll transfer you to Santa Rosa."

Katherine listened to a series of buzzes, clicks, and whirrs before a male voice came on the line.

"This is Ken Sheldon speaking."

"Mr. Sheldon, this is Josh McFadden's wife, Katherine. I need to get in touch with Josh."

The dead silence on the other end of the phone was finally broken by an expulsion of breath.

"Damn," Sheldon said quietly. "I didn't know Josh was married. What lousy timing."

"I beg your pardon?" Katherine wasn't sure she'd heard him right. "Why is it lousy timing to be married?"

"Because you're likely to be a widow, that's why. And soon."

Stunned, Katherine barely registered the bitten-off curse that escaped the man.

"Is Josh in some kind of trouble? Is it the same people from a few weeks ago?"

"Yeah, he's in trouble. And yes, it's probably the same people." Suddenly realizing that he was telling her more than he should, Sheldon turned crisply professional. "Just how much do you know about the project Josh is working on? How much did he tell you?"

"I know that something went wrong and he was knifed." Katherine thought swiftly and decided to stretch the truth. "And I know that he told me to check in after three days. If he hadn't returned, I'm supposed to go after him."

"Go after him?" Sheldon's shock was clear in his startled tones. "There's no way in hell you're going after him! I've been trying to figure a way out of this, and I haven't come up with a single workable plan to get him out. What made him think you could?''

Get him out? Terror gripped Katherine. *Where is he?* She tried to put aside her fear and think rationally. She had to keep Sheldon talking until she found out where Josh was.

"Probably because he knows I have access to certain—unusual—forces," she prevaricated.

"Hah," Sheldon snorted. "Lady, unless you have access to helicopters, explosives, and a crack combat team, it's not gonna make a damn bit of difference."

Katherine thought swiftly. *Helicopters? Explosives? Combat team?* "But I do," she said out loud, her mind quickly running down the list of stuntmen and the equipment at her father's movie location.

"You do?" Sheldon was incredulous. "Who the hell are you, lady?"

"A very determined woman," Katherine said grimly. "How soon can you meet me?"

"Where are you staying?"

She gave him the name of her hotel and he grunted in response.

"I'll be there in ten minutes."

"I'll be waiting."

He hung up without saying good-bye and Katherine sat motionless for a moment, staring at the receiver in her hand and paralyzed with fear, before she forced herself to shake off the numbing inertia and redial the phone.

It took a few moments for the secretary to patch through her call to her father's mobile phone.

"Daddy?" Her voice wobbled and she fought back tears.

"Katy? What's wrong?" Charles Logan's deep voice reflected instant concern.

"Josh is in trouble, and I need you."

"What kind of trouble? Where is he?"

"I don't know." A sob broke her voice and she swallowed another before continuing. "I just know it's something bad."

"All right, honey. I'll be there as fast as I can— probably about twenty minutes."

"Good. Ken Sheldon said it would take him ten minutes to get here."

"Who's Ken Sheldon?"

"I'm not sure, but he knows where Josh is."

"Wait for me—don't leave," Charles warned. He knew little about the exact nature of Josh's work, but he was well aware that agents for the Department of Immigration were occasionally involved in dangerous operations. He didn't want Katherine mixed up in anything dangerous.

"I won't, Dad, but hurry."

"I will. 'Bye, Katy."

Katherine hung up the phone and paced the floor, biting her lip, until it occurred to her that it might be helpful to make a list of the stuntmen working for her father and their specialities.

Ken Sheldon was delayed a few moments by traffic, Charles Logan was faster than he had anticipated, and the two men arrived at Katherine's hotel room within a few minutes of each other.

"Logan?" Ken Sheldon's pale blue eyes narrowed over the distinguished older man's trim figure. "Don't I know that name from somewhere?"

"Could be." Charles smiled faintly. "I make movies."

"Oh, yeah." Sheldon drew out the words, his lips pursing in a silent whistle. His gaze flicked from Charles to Katherine and back. "Well, looks like Josh did all right for himself. Now"—his voice lost its humor and turned deadly serious—"suppose you tell me what kind of forces you have access to."

"What kind do we need?" Katherine asked, gesturing the two men to seats at the small round table near the doors that led out to the balcony.

"Helicopters, explosives, and a SWAT team," Sheldon said bluntly. "You told me on the phone that you had access to them. Do you?"

Katherine looked at her father.

"We do," Charles Logan said calmly, his gaze flicking from his daughter's anxious face to Sheldon's shrewd one. "Where is Josh?"

Sheldon considered them for a moment before reaching a decision. "Confiding in civilians is strictly against departmental policy, but I'm going to level with you. Josh went into the Mexican interior three days ago with two other agents—they had some unfinished business with a smuggler named Castaneda. They should have been back out within seventy-two hours. Their time was up at eight o'clock this morning, and I haven't heard a word from any of them."

"But that was four hours ago! Where are they? Does that mean something went wrong?" Beneath the cover of the tabletop, Katherine gripped her hands together in her lap until they ached.

"It means something went very wrong," Sheldon said bluntly.

"What are you going to do about it?" she demanded. "Have you sent someone after them?"

Sheldon ran agitated fingers through his thick crop

of sandy hair. "I haven't got anyone to send! This chance to nail Castaneda wasn't expected, and those three were the only agents I had in the area. I'd go myself, but I need more than just one man to get them out—I need backup." He didn't add, *if they're still alive*, but the words were implicit and all three of them knew it.

"We'll give you backup, won't we, Dad?" Katherine's eyes pleaded with her father.

Charles Logan had never been able to deny his only daughter. He nodded.

"All you want, Sheldon."

"Good." Sheldon rubbed his hands together in satisfaction. "We need a plan—have you got paper and pens?"

Katherine rose to search for hotel stationery and pens, listening closely as Sheldon questioned her father.

"How many men have you got, and what kind of experience have they had?"

"Twenty-two stuntmen—nearly all of them served in the military. Hal Kinsey and Mike Bonnwell were both Navy Seals. This movie is an action thriller, so I've got a crack crew of stuntmen—the best in the business."

"Castaneda and his gang won't be shooting blanks, you know," Sheldon warned bluntly. "Someone's likely to get hurt—or turn up dead."

"I'll tell them." Charles's eyes crinkled at the corners as his mouth curved in a wry smile. "But knowing that crew of maniacs, I figure they'll probably be all the more eager to go."

"All right, just so you know. Now." Sheldon's beefy fingers began to move over the sheet of paper, drawing a map. "Castaneda's holed up in a dead end canyon that's damn near impossible to get into— that's why we need the helicopter. I figure we can station several sharpshooters along the rim of the canyon and move a small team into the canyon over the western edge. The team can locate our men and get them to the helicopter pad in the center, and the sharpshooters on the rim can keep Castaneda's forces pinned down while our helicopter lands to pick up Josh and the rest of the team and fly them out."

Charles stared consideringly at the rough sketch, mentally reviewing the action necessary to succeed. "It just might work," he said slowly.

"If a team of men can get into the canyon, why can't they get Josh out the same way? Why do we need a helicopter?" Katherine asked.

"Because, going in, they'll have to rappel down the canyon cliff, and they'll have the cover of darkness and the benefit of surprise. But when they go out, that place is going to be lit up like a Christmas tree, and they'd be sitting ducks trying to climb that sheer face. They'd never make it out alive."

"Oh." Katherine had an instant, vivid mental picture of Josh dangling from a rope against a cliff, riddled with bullets, and nausea gripped her.

Neither man noticed her pale face; each was too busy discussing the details of the project. She sat silently, concentrating on listening to the details while they argued over the fine points. At last, they finished and pushed back their chairs.

"We'll leave here at three o'clock, then," Sheldon said, glancing at his watch. "I've got exactly 1:05."

"Right." Charles checked his own watch and made a fractional adjustment.

"It should take us no more than three hours to get to the rendezvous point, which allows us plenty of time to get into position and be ready to move by dark. It's a good thing there won't be a moon tonight." Sheldon gripped Charles's hand in a firm handshake, nodded to Katherine, and abruptly left the room.

Katherine watched her father pick up the telephone, and within seconds, he was barking orders. She didn't have to see the men on the other end to know that they were moving almost before he hung up the phone. She'd seen her father in action before, and knew that his crew trusted him and would move first and ask questions later.

It wasn't until they were loading into the trucks lined up in the alley behind their hotel that Charles realized that Katherine planned to go with them.

"Where do you think you're going?" he demanded, swiftly taking in her serviceable jeans, tennis shoes, and dark shirt.

"With you."

"No, you're not," he said implacably.

"Yes, I am," she said, her jaw firming with the same stubborn resolution.

"It's too dangerous, and you're not going."

"I have to, Dad." She could see the refusal forming on his lips and forestalled him. "Please—I love him. I can't sit here and wait to find out if he's alive or dead. Don't ask me to, please."

Her almost-whispered last words were more than he could withstand.

"All right," he growled, "but don't get in the way. I could never explain it to your mother if I let anything happen to you."

"Thanks, Daddy." She brushed a kiss against his jaw and climbed into his jeep.

Charles drove his company jeep, Ken Sheldon beside him and Katherine in the backseat, at the head of the short column of trucks that left Santa Rosa and headed east beneath the blazing afternoon sun. The local citizens were used to the movie people traveling in caravans and thought nothing of it as the vehicles stirred up a cloud of dust in passing. The helicopters had left a good fifteen minutes earlier to meet them at the rendezvous point.

There was no moonlight. The desert lay still and peaceful beneath the vast vault of sky, lit only by the far-off glitter of stars. Katherine lay flat on her stomach behind a shield of sagebrush, peering down into the canyon from her position on the rim.

The canyon itself was a dead end, and for most travelers, there was only one way in and out. The smugglers had the open end well guarded. The canyon walls were steep and impassable by normal means, the canyon itself so narrow as to be almost inaccessible by all but the most daring of helicopter pilots. The buildings that housed the smugglers were ranged against the near wall, almost directly below Katherine's position, and the small helicopter pad in the center of the canyon floor was empty of vehicles.

"How long will it take them?" Katherine whispered anxiously.

"I don't know," Charles whispered back, his field glasses trained on the brush that grew intermittently down the cliff below them.

Hal Kinsey and Mike Bonnwell had disappeared over the rim of the canyon, rappelling down the cliff on ropes, some fifteen minutes earlier. But it felt like fifteen hours to Katherine.

"They have to find Josh and the other two first," Charles continued in a low voice. He lifted a finger to point to a small shed behind one of the larger buildings where an armed guard leaned against the porch post. "My guess is, they're holding them prisoner in that shed."

"Where? Let me see."

Charles handed her the glasses and she trained them in the direction he pointed. The guard's figure was burly even at this distance, the rifle slung over his shoulder by its strap menacing, and she swallowed, handing the glasses back to her father.

"As soon as they locate Josh and the others and get them out, they'll set off the explosives for a diversion, and to let the helicopter know that they're ready to be picked up."

Katherine looked down at the helicopter pad; it seemed incredibly small and distressingly exposed.

"There's not much cover where the helicopter has to land, is there?" she said softly.

Charles's gaze flicked over her pale face and his hand squeezed hers comfortingly. "There's enough. We'll get him out, honey." He only wished he were as sure of their success as he wanted her to believe. "I wish you'd go back down to the trucks, where it's safe."

"All right."

To his surprise, she agreed. If he'd been less occupied, he would have been suspicious of her meek compliance, but as it was, he only felt relief that she would be out of danger.

Katherine inched backward on elbows, knees, and

toes until she was safely away from the edge of the canyon. Then she got to her feet and ran for the cluster of trucks tucked out of sight and hearing of the canyon. Her destination was the first of the four helicopters parked beyond the trucks. The pilot of the lead helicopter was in his fifties, lean and grizzled, with a full beard shot with silver that matched the mane of hair caught into a ponytail at his nape.

Crouched behind the cover of a clump of sagebrush, Katherine waited until Ralph, the pilot, had finished his preflight check and disappeared around the far side of the big chopper. She rose and, bent double, raced to the helicopter and scrambled aboard, crawling quickly on her hands and knees to the very back of the large compartment.

"What the hell was that?"

She caught her breath and held it as Ralph's deep bass voice growled with suspicion. His boots crunched against the rough ground as he circled the chopper, and Katherine tugged free a blanket from the stack of them she lay against and pulled it over her. Shivering with apprehension, she willed her quivering muscles and shuddering breath to stillness when she heard his footsteps come nearer and stop as he paused to peer into the wide, open door she had scrambled through only moments before.

"Hey, Ralph," a male voice called softly. "They've got 'em. Warm it up."

"Right! We're outta here, Pat."

Katherine heard the two men climb aboard, and then the slowly increasing noise of the blades as they gathered speed. Her stomach lurched as the chopper lifted off the ground and she waited several minutes, until she knew it was too late for them to turn back, before she threw back the blanket and sucked in deep gusts of air into starved lungs.

It was dark inside the helicopter, except for the dash lights that illuminated Ralph's and Pat's faces with a green glow.

Katherine stretched her cramped legs and her toe caught a can, knocking it against the wall with a clatter.

"What the hell . . . !"

Pat looked over his shoulder and his eyes rounded in dismay.

"Kate! What are you doing here?"

Ralph's deep voice turned the air blue with cuss words. "You're not supposed to be in this chopper! I heard your dad tell Sheldon you were staying with the trucks!"

"I couldn't wait back there—I'd go crazy not knowing if Josh was safe or not." *Or dead.* She shoved the words away, refusing to consider that he might not be alive.

"Yeah, well, you're the one that might not be safe! It's too damn late to take you back now. But when we get back on the ground, missy, I'm gonna paddle your rear for this little stunt, just like I did when you were five years old!"

"Yes, Ralph," Katherine said meekly, knowing full well that his bark was worse than his bite.

"You just stay down and out of the way," he ordered.

A rebel yell broke from Pat. "It's show time!"

"Buckle in back there, Kate," Ralph ordered sharply, and the helicopter turned, banking into a curve that would take them directly into the midst of the explosions. "Damn fool woman!" he grumbled.

On the ground, Hal Kinsey lit the first stick of dynamite and tossed it into a storage shed. The resulting blast set off a string of explosions that lit up the night and turned the smuggler's haven into a holocaust. He grinned, gave Mike Bonnwell a thumbs-up sign, and led him and the three other men in the opposite direction, away from the buildings and the half-dressed men spilling out of doorways and toward the sparse cover next to the helicopter pad.

"The chopper will be here in a minute," Hal said, speaking close to Josh's ear to make himself heard above the roar of explosions. "When it touches down, run for it. We've got rifles up on the rim to give us cover."

Josh nodded his head in silent agreement, conserving his strength as his narrowed blue gaze searched the sky for aircraft. When Castaneda had sprung the trap and caught him and the two other agents, he'd known that there was no way Sheldon could get to them in time. Castaneda had spent the day alternately ignoring them and beating them for information and pure vicious pleasure, but within a day or two, the smuggler leader would have tired of the sport and killed them. When the two Americans showed up and pulled the three agents out a back window of the shed, Josh had gone without an argument, figuring that any chance was better than none.

He turned to ask the man beside him how Sheldon had found him, when the whirr of helicopter blades interrupted him.

"Here they come—get ready."

Just as the helicopter hovered and began to drop to the ground, Castaneda discovered the empty shed. Rifle bullets kicked up dirt behind the five.

"Let's go! This is too damn close for comfort!"

They ran, zigzagging across the open ground, dodging the hail of bullets that rained around them, to reach the helicopter. A hand caught Josh's and a brawny arm pulled him aboard, the other four scrambling into the chopper just as it left the canyon floor, rising swiftly.

Josh lay sprawled where he'd landed, facedown on the vibrating floorboards, gasping from the exertion.

"Josh, are you hurt? Josh, answer me!"

The frantic, feminine voice pierced the fog of pain and exhaustion that surrounded him and he rolled his head sideways, his eyes widening in shock as Katherine's face came into view. He flopped over onto his back and stared up at her.

"Katy? What the hell are you doing here?"

"Rescuing you, you idiot! Are you hurt?" Her fingers busily tore at his bloodstained shirt, ripping it open. "Oh, no!" Her eyes in her pale face glittered emerald-bright with tears as her gaze flicked away from the ugly knife wound across his ribs.

Josh tried to smile at her. "Remember that guy who didn't like my face?"

Katherine nodded, sniffing as tears rolled down her cheeks, her fingers frozen into fists over the edges of his shirt.

"Well, he didn't like it any better this time around," Josh joked weakly, before he passed out cold.

ELEVEN.

"I want one thing understood," Josh said sternly, tilting Katherine's face up to his. Her hair fanned across the pristine white of the pillowcase, her cheeks once again flushed with pink color.

"What's that?" she asked, snuggling carefully, contentedly, against his uninjured side.

"You are absolutely never, and I mean *never*, to put yourself in that kind of danger again!"

"But, Joshua," she said, widening her eyes at him with an expression of complete innocence, "nobody got hurt."

"This time nobody got hurt," he growled. "We were lucky, incredibly lucky. If the Department ever finds out that we used a bunch of amateurs to bail us out, we're in deep trouble."

Katherine smoothed her fingertips over the snow-white bandage against his ribs. "Actually, the only one who got hurt was you. The amateurs never even got a scratch."

Josh glared at her. But she was right. The stern lines of his face softened. "Did I tell you how thankful I am that you and that crazy bunch of stuntmen showed up?"

"Yes." She grinned at him. "Only about a hundred times or so."

"Do you know," he said disbelievingly, "they all thanked me."

"They thanked you?" She looked confused. "Why?"

"They said they appreciated the opportunity to have a little fun. Usually they do that kind of stuff for work." Josh eyed her. "Are all movie people nuts, or is it just stuntmen?"

She laughed and dropped a kiss on his cheek. "I'm almost afraid to tell you this, but I think they're all a little crazy—including my father."

"Hmm." Josh shook his head in amazement.

"You shouldn't be worrying about movie people, not when you have me around," she said.

Josh grinned, his blue gaze running with appreciation over her slim curves, covered only by a silk pajama shirt. "Why is that?"

Katherine got to her knees so she could lean threateningly over him. "Because," she said throatily, "I'm going to hold you hostage in this hotel room until you give me everything I want."

"And what do you want?" he asked as she bent closer, the subtle scent of perfume heated by warm woman drifting over him.

"You," she whispered, her lips brushing against his. "I want you."

"You can have me," he murmured, his eyes hot

with the fire that kindled in his body. "Anytime, anyplace."

"Now," she breathed. "I want you now, and tomorrow, and the day after that, and the day after . . ."

His hand caught the back of her head and pulled her close, crushing her mouth against his. But when he moved to roll her beneath him on the bed, pain stabbed through his ribs and he grunted with the fiery reminder.

"What's wrong?" Katherine asked with quick, husky concern. Her fingers flew to his ribs and stroked gently over the white bandage.

"You're going to have to do the taking tonight, honey," he said, resting back against the pillows.

Katherine's breath shortened, her lashes lowering over darkened emerald eyes. "Are you sure we won't hurt you if we make love?"

"Not nearly as much as I'll hurt if we don't make love," he growled, and pulled her down to bury his mouth against hers.

Hours later, they lay against the pillows, watching the balmy Mexican night fading into pink dawn.

"You realize, of course," Katherine said drowsily, sated and sleepy with pleasure, "that I'm not going to file for divorce. You're stuck with me, McFadden."

Eyes closed, Josh smiled, his lips curving against the silky crown of her head. "Yeah, I guess you're right. Only you've got it wrong, honey—it's you who's stuck with me. I got the best of this bargain."

"Silly man," she said, yawning daintily. A sudden thought occurred to her and she half opened her eyes to look up at him. "I told your mother that you're thinking of moving back to CastleRock to work with Mark Daly.''

"What did she say?''

"She was delighted,'' Katherine said, a smile curving her mouth.

"So am I, honey, so am I.'' Josh held her as she fell asleep and drifted off to sleep himself to dreams of an old Victorian house on a shady street and Katherine waiting on the porch when he came home from work. Settling down and ceasing traveling suddenly seemed the best of all worlds.

SHARE THE FUN . . .
SHARE YOUR NEW-FOUND TREASURE!!

You don't want to let your new books out of your sight?
That's okay. Your friends can get their own. Order below.

No.   4 WINTERFIRE by Lois Faye Dyer
Beautiful NY model and rugged Idaho rancher find their own magic.

No.   21 THAT JAMES BOY by Lois Faye Dyer
Jesse believes in love at first sight. Will he convince Sarah?

No.   70 SUNDAY KIND OF LOVE by Lois Faye Dyer
Trace literally sweeps beautiful, ebony-haired Lily off her feet.

No.   88 MORE THAN A MEMORY by Lois Faye Dyer
Cole and Melanie both still burn from the heat of that long ago summer.

No. 106 TRAVELIN' MAN by Lois Faye Dyer
Josh needs a temporary bride. The ruse is over, can he let her go?

No.   89 JUST ONE KISS by Carole Dean
Michael is Nikki's guardian angel and too handsome for his own good.

No.   90 HOLD BACK THE NIGHT by Sandra Steffen
Shane is a man with a mission and ready for anything . . . except Starr.

No.   91 FIRST MATE by Susan Macias
It only takes a minute for Mac to see that Amy isn't so little anymore.

No.   92 TO LOVE AGAIN by Dana Lynn Hites
Cord thought just one kiss would be enough. But Honey proved him wrong!

No.   93 NO LIMIT TO LOVE by Kate Freiman
Lisa was called the "little boss" and Bruiser didn't like it one bit!

No.   94 SPECIAL EFFECTS by Jo Leigh
Catlin wouldn't fall for any tricks from Luke, the master of illusion.

No.   95 PURE INSTINCT by Ellen Fletcher
She tried but Amie couldn't forget Buck's strong arms and teasing lips.

No.   96 THERE IS A SEASON by Phyllis Houseman
The heat of the volcano rivaled the passion between Joshua and Beth.

No.   97 THE STILLMAN CURSE by Peggy Morse
Leandra thought revenge would be sweet. Todd had sweeter things in mind.

No.   98 BABY MAKES FIVE by Lacey Dancer
Cait could say 'no' to his business offer but not to Robert, the man.

No.   99 MOON SHOWERS by Laura Phillips
Both Sam and the historic Missouri home quickly won Hilary's heart.

No. 100 GARDEN OF FANTASY by Karen Rose Smith
If Beth wasn't careful, she'd fall into the arms of her enemy, Nash.

No. 101 HEARTSONG by Judi Lind
From the beginning, Matt knew Lainie wasn't a run-of-the-mill guest.

No. 102 SWEPT AWAY by Cay David
Sam was insufferable . . . and the most irresistible man Charlotte ever met.

No. 103 FOR THE THRILL by Janis Reams Hudson
Maggie hates cowboys, *all* cowboys! Alex has his work cut out for him.

No. 104 SWEET HARVEST by Lisa Ann Verge
Amanda never mixes business with pleasure but Garrick has other ideas.

No. 105 SARA'S FAMILY by Ann Justice
Harrison always gets his own way . . . until he meets stubborn Sara.

No. 107 STOLEN KISSES by Sally Falcon
In Jessie's search for Mr. Right, Trevor was definitely a wrong turn!

No. 108 IN YOUR DREAMS by Lynn Bulock
Meg's dreams become reality when Alex reappears in her peaceful life.

Meteor Publishing Corporation
Dept. 992, P. O. Box 41820, Philadelphia, PA 19101-9828

Please send the books I've indicated below. Check or money order (U.S. Dollars only)—no cash, stamps or C.O.D.s (PA residents, add 6% sales tax). I am enclosing $2.95 plus 75¢ handling fee for *each* book ordered.

Total Amount Enclosed: $_____.

____ No. 4	____ No. 90	____ No. 96	____ No. 102
____ No. 21	____ No. 91	____ No. 97	____ No. 103
____ No. 70	____ No. 92	____ No. 98	____ No. 104
____ No. 88	____ No. 93	____ No. 99	____ No. 105
____ No. 106	____ No. 94	____ No. 100	____ No. 107
____ No. 89	____ No. 95	____ No. 101	____ No. 108

Please Print:
Name _____
Address _____ Apt. No. _____
City/State _____ Zip _____

Allow four to six weeks for delivery. Quantities limited.